Victoria Marmot
and the
Dragon's Rage

Virginia McClain

Cover design by Natasha Snow

Works by Virginia McClain

The Victoria Marmot series:

The Chronicles of Gensokai series:

Short Stories

To Mom, for never giving up.

THE ALLEY WAS as dark as an elephant's asshole. I mean, not that I'm super familiar with an elephant's asshole or anything, but you know… it'd be dark, probably, and wet, and smell like feces, so… pretty close to the alley I was currently standing in. Although I'd wager that the elephant would have to be in extremely ill health to have as much standing water lying around inside of it as this alley did. Ok, the simile falls apart at some point, so sue me. I'm not a writer, I'm just a teenager.

Well, "just" may not be the best qualifier for someone who can turn into a snow leopard and also a dragon but… Gwendamnit, narrating is hard.

Look, the alley was dark and wet and I was standing there, surrounded by concrete and refuse, looking around like a dazed meerkat, wishing I had a wand or some shit, so that I could just tap a brick and disappear into Diagon Alley or whatever, but no. Nothing in my life was that easy. There was no wand, there was no half-giant to show me the ropes, there was just me and elephant-ass alley, and a weird tingly feeling in the skin of my hands that got stronger in certain directions and weaker in others. Hence, why I was doing a slow-motion, arrhythmic version of thriller.

As I stepped in yet another puddle and my nostrils informed me that it was a puddle comprised almost entirely of human urine with perhaps a sprinkling of vomit, I decided that I really wasn't a city person.

"Any luck, Gatita?" came a voice from farther down the alley.

"Depends," I said, trying not to retch as I took in enough air to speak, "on what you mean by luck. If you mean have I found the seam, then no. If you mean have I stepped in a statistically disproportionate amount of human excrement? Then yes. Yes, lots of luck."

Sol laughed, and I smiled at the sound, even if nothing else about this scenario was amusing to me.

"You're awfully squeamish for an outdoors-woman."

"Fuck that," I said, turning to glare in Sol's direction, even though it was too dark to see her from where I stood. "I will pick up scat and rub it in my hands to tell you how long ago the nearest mountain lion passed by, sew a gaping wound shut with nothing but a hotel sewing kit, and make a tourniquet out of sticks to set a protruding bone back in place, if I have to. But humans in the city are fucking gross."

For some reason that made Sol laugh even louder.

"I won't argue with that, but I think we're gross everywhere. It's just that there are more of us in the city."

Which was a fair point, and really, La Paz seemed to be no grosser than any other city I'd ever been in—if anything it was cleaner than a few I'd visited—but that wasn't a point my urine-coated self was willing to concede at the moment. Sol had grown up in La Paz, and had an easy confidence here that I envied at times. I could lead us through the remote parts of the Andes that sheltered her family cabin, and the Colorado Rockies might as well have been my backyard, but I was… less useful in the hustle and bustle of just under a million people.

"La Paz isn't even that big," Sol said, walking over to stand between me and yet another nondescript stretch of concrete wall. "It's about the same size as where you lived in Colorado, isn't it?"

I shrugged.

"I'm pretty sure it's got more people than where I'm from, but even if it doesn't… the Front Range is more like a giant suburb. There isn't much urban center. The population is all spread out. This is different," I explained, gesturing at the narrow alley that contained us, a dumpster, and too many pools of urine. Seeing Sol start to look defensive, I quickly added, "Don't get me wrong, La Paz is beautiful. What little I've seen of it outside this alley is charming, and I'm really looking forward to seeing more of it, but… I'm not a fan of dark, stank alleys, I guess."

Sol ran her hand along my arm, or the black leather that covered it, anyway. I wasn't always in agreement with the style choices of whatever Gwen-granted magic was in charge of supplying new clothes to me (and all the shifters in my immediate vicinity) every time I shifted, but at least it had taken into account that spring in the Andes was no time to leave me in less than a thick leather biker jacket, a pair of lined jeans, and some sturdy boots. The outfit struck me as fairly cliché given that I was standing in a dark alley, could turn into an animal, and occasionally fought vampires, but at least it was warm. All thoughts of my wardrobe fled when Sol leaned in to purr at my ear, though.

"There's a lot that can be accomplished in a dark alley," she whispered, licking my neck and making my skin ignite.

The heat was quickly quelled by the stench of human feces and urine that permeated the place, but it was a testament to how attractive I found Sol that she was able to turn me on even for a moment in those conditions.

"I'm afraid my nose is entirely too sensitive for that to be a pleasant prospect," I replied, disappointed that it was true. "But once we get out of this place I'd be keen to take you up on the offer."

She bit my earlobe playfully.

"Excellent. We haven't had nearly enough time alone for my liking," she purred.

I took a deep breath and tried to swallow. The stench of the alley was becoming less and less of a deterrent the more Sol's breath caressed my neck, and for a moment I was oddly glad that Seamus had decided to go check on his Moms today.

It wasn't that I didn't want Seamus with us on this mission. It was just that I was glad he would be safe for once. He wasn't much of a fighter, after all, and well… at this exact moment… I was ok with Sol having me all to herself.

"Yeah, saving the world is a real buzz kill," I muttered, as I felt my back push up against the concrete wall behind me.

"Yet one more reason that Rebecca Dryer deserves to die," Sol replied, the corner of her lush mouth turning up on one side.

I laughed, because the alternative was to have a full-on panic attack triggered by thinking about how close we were to losing everything.

A few hours ago, when Sol and I had been getting briefed by Trev on what little he could tell us about Rhelia's mission—basically that Torrence was a potential contact and that she had gone dark earlier after her morning check in—we'd been interrupted by a series of newsflashes about demands being made from the "unknown terrorist organization in Sucre."

Apparently, Rebecca Dryer wasn't feeling patient, and she was already making demands that the U.N. cede power to her, along with all the nations that weren't members of the U.N. She was threatening to set off more "weapons of mass destruction" if her demands weren't met in the next 48 hours. That had been eight hours ago, and, unfortunately, Dryer wasn't saying *where* she was planning to do her mass destruction. Con-sequently, we were left without any leads, despite Trev and Rhelia having gone sleepless hacking and monitoring every bit of MOME security footage they could get their code on for the past two days. None of the backup footage they'd managed to access had turned up anything useful regarding our two missing weredragons yet.

The people we loved, our homes, the Earth… maybe even the whole universe were at stake here, and we were out of time for anything but drastic measures. To top it off, Rhelia had been following a desperate lead when she'd suddenly gone dark.

Which had me swallowing for an entirely different reason, trying to keep the emotion at bay. Everyone I had left, which was a pretty short list these days, had come far too close to death already in the past three weeks for my liking.

For some reason—sympathy, empathy, a sudden need to remind us both that there was still some good in the world—Sol took that moment to pull me close and kiss me deeply. For the span of a few heartbeats I was consumed by the fire of that kiss and everything else was swept away; it didn't matter that the Ministry of Magical Entities was trying to kill us, that they were holding the world hostage with a potentially Earth-annihilating weapon, that my brother was still barely talking to me after it had looked like I'd killed his mate two days ago in order to save all of our lives. Those thoughts had consumed me five seconds ago, but in that moment they ceased to exist.

Elephant asshole and all, I *really* didn't want to pull away from that kiss, but the tingling in my hands wouldn't let up and, eventually, I pulled back just enough to say, "I think I can tell where that seam is."

"**R**EMIND ME WHY we think this is a good idea, Gatita?"

I lowered my hands from where I'd raised them to Sol's shoulders, and stared at her as she leveled her gold-green eyes at me, the graffiti-tagged alley fading away as her eyes caught mine.

"What in particular do you mean?" I asked. "I'm pretty sure my entire life has been one bad idea after another for the past three weeks."

Sol's lips quirked up at the sides, but her gaze remained implacable.

"I mean, why do we think that going to Unterberg is a worthwhile use of our time? I still think that we'd be better off waiting for a lead from your brother or—"

"My brother basically admitted that he was out of leads, Sol, not to mention out of options, as soon as Rhelia didn't check in this afternoon." I reminded her, before she could get caught up in the same argument she'd had with Trev before we left. "If all the surveillance he's doing isn't getting us anywhere, then whatever long shot Rhelia is taking is the only chance we've got right now. He's trying to sort through security footage from five different MOME HQs and who knows how many smaller outposts. Even if he had a whole team working for him it would take days to find anything useful. We just don't have the time."

"But Dryer could use Siara as her next bomb at any moment, and we don't even know what lead Rhelia was following when she left this morning."

Sol's voice was marked by the frustration we'd all been feeling since we'd sat helplessly by and watched a whole section of Sucre get razed to the ground three days ago (or in my case, watched the news reports of it after I'd regained consciousness). That frustration had started leaning heavily towards terror as we'd watched the morning news flash headlines about demands from the mysterious terrorist organization that was responsible for the attacks. Of course, we knew exactly what the "mysterious" terrorist organization was, but that didn't help anything. The fact that we knew that the organization was MOME, and that we knew that MOME was being led by Rebecca Dryer in this particular mission did us little good since we didn't know where Rebecca Dryer was, or, more importantly, where she was holding the two weredragons that she was intending to use as her next weapons of mass destruction.

"We know Rhelia thought whatever lead she had was our only chance to find Siara and Emil before they wind up turned into Hiroshima and Nagasaki times a bajillion, so I'm inclined to think that her mission, whatever it is, has become priority number one," I said, trying to keep the irritation out of my voice. I didn't succeed.

"But Dryer could use anyone as a bomb now. Why are we even going after Siara and Emil when Dryer could explode any of her own agents if she felt like it? Shouldn't we just be planning to take out all of MOME now? I know the dragons supposedly make the biggest bang, but does that really mean that they won't use someone else even if we manage to get Siara and Emil back from them? Gatita, I know you trust your brother and Rhelia, but…" her voice trailed off and she shrugged, leaving me to fill in the blanks.

I bristled. I understood perfectly what she was getting at, and I didn't want to hear it.

"You think it hasn't occurred to me more than once that Trev was in MOME custody for over a decade?" I hissed. Just because it was a possibility I'd considered myself, didn't mean it was one that I wanted to talk about. Something Sol had assuredly picked up on when she'd brought it up while I was still recovering from my own injuries. Rhelia had still been pretending to be dead to everyone but me and Trev, and Trev had seemed oddly distant. He still did. It was disconcerting to all of us, especially me, but what did any of us expect when it had basically looked to him like his sister had killed his mate right in front of his eyes?

"You worked for MOME for three years," I said, latching on to whatever I could to avoid talking or thinking about the idea of not trusting my twin. "You could be loyal to them just as easily as Trev could."

Sol's eyes flashed and her lips formed a hard line, all hints of humor vanishing in a breath.

"They killed my mother, my aunt, and my cousin," she said, her voice a harsh whisper. "Do you think that made me loyal?"

I took a deep breath, but it still felt like I'd been punched in the stomach. Sol had been more than a little reluctant to talk about what MOME had done to her family, and who she had lost. This was the first time I'd heard her say who was killed. I was suddenly swamped with sadness, not just for Sol and her family, but for Trev and everything he'd been through, for all of us who MOME had fucked with and tried to destroy.

Taking a deep breath, I reminded myself that we'd all been under a metric shit-ton of stress lately and that neither of us was in a great headspace right now.

"And they killed Trev's parents, abducted him as a child, and have been trying to kill him, me, and his mate, ever since he finally got away from them," I replied. "What loyalty do you expect him to have for them?"

I had hoped that the grief I was feeling for all of us would show through my voice enough to disarm Sol, but I should have known better. Her voice was still icy when she spoke again.

"You said yourself he was a child when they took him," Sol began. "He was more susceptible to—"

"And how old were you when they took your family from you?" I was losing my patience despite everything Sol had just admitted to me.

"That's different!" she countered. "I wasn't trapped with MOME after that, I didn't have a chance to develop Stockholm Syndrome or to—"

"Look. Even if you think that Trev would betray us, do you really think that we're so crucial to the dragons' resistance plans that misdirecting us is going to bring the whole thing crashing down?" I couldn't believe I was having to have this argument for the second time today.

"We may not be, but Rhelia is one of—"

"Rhelia left this morning to go on this mission despite Trev's best arguments against it, because she was convinced that she knew something the rest of us didn't that would help us find Siara and Emil, even if she couldn't tell us what that was. If Trev was secretly trying to help MOME, he either wouldn't have tried to stop her, or he wouldn't be sending us to help her now. You can't have it both ways, Sol."

"It just seems dangerous to head to Unterberg right now, considering everything that happened to us the last time we went there. And the time before that."

That was hard to argue with, but I tried anyway.

"Is there anywhere in the universe that's safe for us right now?" I asked, almost ready to collapse against the brick wall behind me. I probably would have, if I hadn't been convinced it was covered in human urine.

Sol finally laughed, and I could only stare at her as though her head had suddenly grown horns.

"You're right, Gatita," she sighed, running a hand along my arm again. It felt like a magnet pulling all the tension out of my body. "That's probably why I'm feeling so combative. We aren't safe anywhere, and we haven't been for so long, I'm starting to feel a bit frayed around the edges. I kinda desperately wish we had time to spar."

It was difficult to keep myself from angling my head at Sol like puppy that had just seen a large hoppy bug.

"WHY HAVEN'T WE BEEN SPARRING!?" I asked, grabbing Sol by both arms.

She laughed again and this time I joined her.

"Maybe because we've been fighting real bad guys nonstop since we met?" she suggested.

"Yeah, good point. Fine, but when this is all over, we're definitely sparring."

"Maybe once we find Rhelia and use her secret plan to retrieve our missing weredragons."

It was a sobering reminder that we rather desperately needed to be elsewhere, not here, making out and debating our orders, surrounded by human waste.

I sighed.

The last seam we had used to sneak into Unterberg had been compromised immediately after we'd used it, so we had to assume MOME was watching it. The dragons had a secondary seam that was safe enough for Seamus to sneak in and visit his Moms, but it let out in a public square and was still too public for a top-secret rescue mission— or whatever this was. We needed a new seam that wasn't monitored by MOME, but also dropped out somewhere a bit more circumspect.

Luckily for us, there were a lot of seams to Unterberg. Unluckily for us, most of the ones MOME didn't know about were little more than rumors in dark bars. It had taken us all day to find a trustworthy(ish) source in a dingy cafe in La Paz. Then it had taken us a few more hours to find the nondescript back alley our less than sober source had described, let alone the seam itself.

Rhelia had mentioned to Trev that she might need some backup not long after she'd arrived in Unterberg, and then she'd missed her midday check-in. Trev couldn't go, because he was knee deep in security feeds from all of MOME's bases of operation, trying to find our missing weredragons, and the only person qualified to do the job instead of him was Rhelia. Despite that, he'd practically begged to come with us. He'd been a wreck ever since Rhelia had failed to check in, and the only way I'd convinced him to stay behind was to remind him that if Rhelia headed back to the Dragon Realm while we were gone he'd miss her, and if he missed a chance to locate Siara and Emil while we were gone, Rhelia would tear him in two.

So he'd stayed, and we'd left, and you, dear reader, (assuming I buy Gwen's whole, "I'm supposed to be your narrator, you're in a book," line) caught up with us making out in an alley in La Paz.

But just before we'd started arguing, the Marco Polo game my hands had been playing with whatever it was in seams that made my skin vibrate had come to an abrupt halt as I had been running them up Sol's back. As I had reached her shoulders, I'd suddenly realized that the reason I'd been going back and forth through this urban shit funnel without finding anything was that the pull I kept feeling wasn't coming from in front of me or behind me, as I'd initially suspected, but from directly above me, instead.

And, indeed, when—deciding that Sol's laughter and dropping of the topic of Trev-as-Traitor meant that she'd agreed we could move on with our mission—I finally stretched my hands into the air, I felt like I was parting a curtain.

"If you don't think Unterberg is too dangerous," I said, with as much scathing sarcasm as I could muster, "grab on."

Then I dropped into a crouch, and Sol complied, asking no questions, but throwing me a startled look.

Not nearly as startled as I probably looked when I fell on my ass a second later, after attempting to hop into the air with a hundred and twenty pound person on my back, and instead collapsing in a small heap of pain, embarrassment, and unfortunate bodily fluids.

"What were you trying to do, exactly?" Sol asked, as we attempted to brush the dripping human excrement from our clothes.

"The seam is above us. We need to launch ourselves upwards."

"And you thought you were going to launch us both six feet into the air using nothing but your human form?"

I muttered something indecipherable and shuffled my feet, staring fixedly at a patch of filth on my jeans.

"How about we shift first?" Sol suggested, rather politely not mentioning how idiotic my initial plan had been.

"How will you hold onto me?"

"You know I don't actually have to hold you to pass through a seam, right? That's why we're using a seam instead of having you use your Gwen-given-power to shift us there, remember? So you don't tire before we even know what we're up against."

That was news to me. I mean, it shouldn't have been. We'd talked about using seams instead of me shifting us to save energy, I just... had we talked about how anyone could use a seam if they already knew where it was? The more I thought about it, the more I suspected we had. Because I was now remembering Sol telling me how sometimes even non-magical folks walk through them by accident and that's where you get your Narnia and Wonderland type scenarios. I clearly needed more sleep. It hadn't been an easy... month.

Not wanting to drag out what was quickly becoming a thoroughly embarrassing conversation for me, I decided to focus on shifting. I imagined what it felt like to have a tail for counterbalance, a much lower center of gravity, and whiskers wide enough to help me navigate swiftly through cracks in rock. Then, almost instantly, I felt myself take on my feline form.

Damn, it feels good to be a snow leopard.

At the same time, Sol took shape as a large panther beside me, and I gave her one quick nod before launching myself at the magic I had sensed with my fingers. A magic that now took on a full-body, physical sensation, as my furry form collided with what felt like a large velvet drape lined with hot taffy.

~~~

"Woah," I whispered, as we shifted back to human immediately upon hitting the cobbles of a very different alley in a very different city. La Paz's 16th century colonial charm (if we want to call colonialism charming—which was not at all high on my list of things to call colonialism; I had some other choice words for colonialism that were far less complimentary—but if we're just talking architecture, sure, the buildings were cute) had been left behind and replaced with a sort of melted glass meets Sagrada Familia look that was so impressive it left me with the vocabulary of Keanu Reeves learning Kung-fu.

The last time I'd been in this city we'd been instantly set upon by MOME agents and then apprehended by the Unterberg security golems (who had promptly put bags over our heads), so I hadn't had
~~~

much time to look around, even though I'd been just as entranced with the view then as now.

Instead of the scent of alley sewage (thankfully shed along with our clothes, which had been replaced due to our brief stint in feline form), the air here was filled with something warm and slightly floral, as though fruit-bearing trees were in bloom nearby—albeit no tree I was familiar with. Indeed, peeking above a high wall nearby, visible even in the moonlight, their blossoms were a riot of colors rarely seen in my world, striped and polka dotted as though they were more fashion show that flower. The buildings looked almost organic, aside from the fact that they followed patterns that looked so intricate and symmetrical it was difficult to imagine that they weren't created by sentient beings. The color selections also seemed too vibrant and contrasting to be naturally occurring. While most of the architecture seemed to be made of stone or clay, every building was adorned with giant sections of glass—windows and sometimes entire walls—forming a vibrant display that reflected even the moonlight with enthusiasm.

As we walked from the cobbled alley where we'd arrived into the larger, cobbled street beyond, it was difficult for me not to stare. The streets, which had been packed with people headed to market the last time we had been here, seemed no less crowded now that the sun was down. The people were almost impossible to describe, and en-compassed beings whose skin colors ranged from lime to aubergine, jet black to glittering silver, and who sported a startling array of hair, fins, wings, and horns, not to mention a variety of limb numbers that often exceeded four. I couldn't help but smile, as I turned to Sol and reached for her hand.

"Unterberg may not be safe, but at least the sightseeing is good when you aren't instantly forced to run for your life," I said.

Which was, of course, when a large, black ball of fur launched itself at me, tackling me against the nearest decorative window before I could even make out where it had come from.

"WHAT THE FUCK? Seamus?" I said, as the black ball of fur disengaged from my chest to shift back to his human form, complete with a jeans and T-shirt combo appropriate for Unterberg's warm summer nights. Unfortunately, I was too flustered from having my back abruptly slammed into an ornate stained-glass window to appreciate the way the aforementioned T-shirt clung to his swimmer's body, the way he smelled slightly of fur and cinnamon, or the way the moonlight glinted off his amber eyes.

"What are you doing here?" I asked.

"It's uh… a long story," Seamus said, looking somewhat abashedly from Sol to me. "I was worried about you two."

I took a deep breath and tried not to let out an exasperated sigh. We'd all been worried about each other lately, but Seamus had been safely tucked away with his Moms for once, and I had been mildly relieved to think he wouldn't be risking his ass with us today.

"Seamus, I thought we talked about the over-protective male thing," I began, but Seamus cut me off.

"It's not that, Vic. Fuck's sake, you're here with Sol. I know you two can take care of yourselves better than I can."

Seamus' eyes darkened and I wondered if he was angry or jealous about that fact.

"So, what's going on? Is everyone ok?"

Seamus took a deep breath.

"My Moms are fine, if that's what you're asking, but…"

To my surprise it was Sol who took Seamus' arm and turned him so that she could look in his eyes and speak to him with a level of concern I hadn't heard from her before.

"Did you see something?" she asked.

Seamus looked like he might cry with relief as he nodded, and I kicked myself for jumping to the assumption that he was here to play the overbear-ing male in a story that had far too many alphas in it already. I should have known better. Seamus might have a protective streak from being a wolf raised by wolves, but he had little interest in dominance. He must have had a vision.

"Do you want to tell us about it?" I asked, belatedly trying to match Sol's level of concern.

Seamus shook his head and took a deep breath.

"I don't think I should. Not all of it, at least. First, because we don't really have time, and second…" Seamus looked between both of us, as though he was searching for an answer to a question he hadn't asked aloud. I didn't know what answer he was looking for, so I just smiled as reassuringly as I could while Sol squeezed his arm a bit. "Don't freak out, but Rhelia needs our help. Which I suppose you guys know if you're here already, but… I need to be there too, and… this is gonna sound weird, but… we can't trust the green lady."

He flinched after he said all of that, as if expecting us to say or do something that would hurt him, now that he'd said it. I just looked between Sol and Seamus and wondered what my life had become that vague prophecies not only didn't surprise me anymore, but kinda made sense. I mean, I didn't know who the green lady was, but whatever, we were in Unterberg, where every color in the Crayola box was a perfectly normal skin tone. Still, I was guessing she'd be pretty obvious when we ran into her. Meanwhile, I was adding to the mental list of questions I needed to ask Seamus when we finally had time to talk like normal humans. Like why he looked like he expected to be punished for telling us about a vision.

"Alright, noted. We won't trust the green lady. Anything else?" I asked.

Seamus shook his head, but there was still a haunted look in his eyes.

"Seamus, are you… are you sure you need to come with us? We have no idea what we're up against here and…"

I trailed off as I realized I was being a colossal hypocrite, after I'd just accused Seamus of being an overprotective git, but… he already looked scared enough to crap his pants, and we all knew that he wasn't a very effective fighter. Maybe I was just trigger shy after almost losing everyone I loved three days ago, but it seemed irresponsible to let him join us on this particular mission if he didn't absolutely have to be there.

Seamus rolled his eyes, and I cringed, expecting him to tell me off for being an ass. Instead he said something completely reasonable.

"Vic, I know I'm not the best fighter. This isn't about that. I just… I have more information than you do, and I can't convey it all in a reasonable amount of time. There are too many variables, and... look, let's just say that when I tried to run alternate scenarios for the future, all the ones without me in them ended... unacceptably."

The amount of times Seamus hesitated in that little speech had me incredibly wary of what he'd seen, but I barely got a chance to pick one of the thousand questions it raised (to start with: Seamus' Moms' new place was on the other side of the city from where we were, and Seamus shouldn't have known where to find us—because we hadn't told anyone how we were getting to Unterberg or where we'd come out; then there was the fact that he could apparently sift through possible futures to see which ones worked best, and the implications of that were off the hook) let alone voice one.

"Seamus, how did you even get—"
I was cut off by a large, heavy hand falling onto my shoulder while a voice said, "You should not be here, Ms. Marmot."

NFORTUNATELY FOR THE body attached to that hand, I don't take kindly to being touched without permission and, unlike a minute ago when I'd been bowled into by a close friend at high velocity, whoever had their hand on my arm was not someone I recognized immediately. Nor did they move fast enough to prevent years of training from kicking in.

Which was how I wound up looking down at the profile of a very large, fur-covered, irate person with a bull's head pressed sideways into the cobblestone street. I was still holding his wrist and twisting it in a way that was designed to be in-credibly painful, which, combined with the impact from rolling over my shoulder and hitting the ground from a few feet up, probably explained the "irate" part of that description.

"Sorry, umm…. Torrence, was it?"

Don't ask me how my brain supplied the name of a minotaur I'd met once in a room full of other fantastic creatures during our first visit here, but… well, to be honest, Torrence is a pretty memorable name. Especially for someone with a bull's head.

Since I remembered him now, and he didn't appear to be trying to kill me at the moment, I released my hold on his arm and helped him to his feet. It took almost a minute before he was able to speak again, though. I guess I'd knocked the wind out of him.

While we waited, I looked to Seamus and Sol, and found that Seamus looked weirdly calm, as though large bull-people regularly put their hands on his friends and wound up lying on the pavement for it. Sol, meanwhile, looked rather like she'd have preferred it if I'd pulled a knife on the guy instead of helping him to his feet.

I shrugged and took a second to look around the crowded street, worried we might have drawn someone's attention and would shortly wind up with a bunch of the council's golems chasing us down again, but it looked like the nighttime hustle of Unterberg remained content to ignore our existence.

"I am sorry if I startled you," Torrence said, when he had finally caught his breath.

I blinked a few times as my brain caught up with what I was hearing. Judging by how pissed Torrence had looked when I'd flipped him, I really hadn't expected an apology.

"Apology accepted. For the record, I do not appreciate being touched without warning or my consent."

Torrence tipped his large bull's head, and the red-brown fur coating his highly sculpted, shirtless upper body glistened a bit in the moonlight.

"Duly noted, Ms. Marmot. I regret the breach of personal space. I was… upset, and not thinking clearly."

I nodded, totally at a loss for words as this mysterious semi-bovine person replied to me with the kind of respect I would hope to get from a 21st century modern human who had overstepped their bounds. Of course, he was a 21st century modern bovine-person. After a moment's consideration, I decided I probably shouldn't let the elements of this place, which reminded me of so many fantasy novels, movies, and MMORPGs, lead me to unfair assumptions about its residents' standards for decency.

As part of my brain reassessed where Torrence (and perhaps all of Unterberg) stood in terms of modern ethics, some other part of my higher functioning raised a more pertinent issue.

"As dragon kin I have the freedom to wander Unterberg in safety," I said, eyeing the minotaur (or tauren, or whatever he was) with a bit more suspicion. "You and the rest of your council left us free to go. Why shouldn't I be here?"

"It isn't safe to discuss out in the open," Torrence whispered. "Would you and your partners be willing to accompany me to a safe location?"

I looked at Sol and Seamus. Sol shrugged, still looking suspicious but not quite as stabby as she had a minute ago. Seamus gave me the kind of nod that told me he had expected this turn of events. I swallowed the questions that sprang to my lips. Now wasn't the time to grill Seamus on how his visions worked, or how much of the future he actually saw, especially considering the fact that Torrence was here, but I made a mental note to ask Seamus all about it the next time we had five minutes to ourselves.

"Fine, Torrence. After you."

"It would be easiest if you would allow me to transport you there."

Honestly, if Rhelia hadn't mentioned Torrence as a contact in her missive to Trevor I never would have agreed, but Seamus had the composed face of someone who wasn't the least bit surprised, and outside of hoping we'd find Rhelia in her apartment, we didn't really have much of a plan now that we'd made it to Unterberg. Whatever info Torrence had would probably be useful, and either way, we certainly didn't want to discuss our mission out in the street.

The bull-man (minotaur? Tauren? I seriously needed a couple minutes with no one trying to kill me so that I could figure what all the major species in Unterberg were called) nodded, straightened himself out while wincing a bit, threaded one of his arms through mine, and then grabbed onto both Sol and Seamus by the forearms, all while saying something guttural that sounded suspiciously like an expletive.

Then the world disappeared.

"UGH... SHIFTING HAS never made me want to throw up before," I muttered, even as my stomach came entirely too close to re-leasing itself on the highly polished marble floor in front of my face.

The floor was in front of my face because I was bent over at the waist trying to hold my dinner in place. I barely registered that it didn't match the cobbled streets we'd been standing on moments ago, because the sounds of Sol failing to keep her own meals in place threatened to overwhelm me. Seamus was also making retching sounds, but as far as I could tell he wasn't actually evacuating his stomach yet. I was doing my best not to breathe through my nose, but a hint of vomit and floor polish trickled in regardless, making the retention of my most recent meals seem less and less likely.

"Strange," said the deep voice that I now associated with the bull's head and heavily furred and muscled torso known as Torrence.

I supposed there were probably some legs involved in the equation, but I really couldn't call them to mind in that moment, as I stared at a particularly shiny vein of marble and tried to think about anything but vomit. That might've been because Torrence was shirtless, or… yeah, ok, maybe because of the bull's head. I mean, the overall effect was pretty distracting. Half because he was surprisingly attractive, bull's head and all, and half because he was a bit disturbing. I mean, don't get me wrong, I can turn into a snow leopard and a dragon, so who the fuck am I to judge someone for having a bull's head, but… it was the transition from what was essentially a very furry human to a full-on bovine head with horns that threw me off, ok? I was trying not to be judgy about it, but it was something I'd only ever seen in video games and movies up to now and… well, seeing it in real life took some getting used to. For me anyway, but hey, add it to the pile, right? What wasn't new to me these days? And Gwendamnit, I must've been desperate to think about anything other than being sick all over this fancy marble if I was this obsessed with Torrence's appearance.

Torrence was mid-way through a sentence my brain hadn't processed at all when he danced out of the range of Sol's latest splatter and straight into my line of sight, drawing my vision from the sparkly, gold-veined marble tiles to some very shapely furred calves and…

"Hooves," I muttered, even as Torrence continued speaking. I had to drag my eyes away from the badass leather kilt that stopped just above Torrence's knee and circled his waist, which was muscular enough that I could make out his six pack even through all the fur. I shook my head and made a stronger effort to tune into what Torrence was saying.

"Most magic users find shifting planes to be both exhausting and nauseating in the early days, and shifters spend their entire lives feeling adverse effects from it. And yet you claim you do not feel it?"

"Nope. I do not claim that at all. I'm just barely not covering your pretty little hooves in the last 24 hours' worth of meals I've eaten. But whenever I shift us, I don't feel this way." Torrence's hooves weren't little, actually, but they were well-kempt and even a bit shiny, so I felt like pretty covered those bases nicely.

Sol kicked me, belatedly, from where she lay crumpled on the floor, and almost toppled into her own vomit. Consequently, I straightened up and went to grab her, hoping to prevent the whole scene from devolving into one of my worst nightmares. No way was I going to keep any food down if she tumbled into a pool of vomit. Just the smell of what was already there was pushing my limits.

Ugh…. Time for a subject change.

"So, what exactly did you just do to us?" I asked, deciding that if Sol wanted me to stop talking about my shifting power, asking my own questions was as good a distraction as any. Not that I thought Torrence would fall for it, but I was genuinely curious anyway.

"He cast a spell, Vic," Sol muttered, her voice still ragged from her recent escapades in food relocation.

"I used my own access to dark matter to pull us through a pocket dimension that paralleled both the location we were in and this location."

"Like lining up stitches in a crochet pattern and then pulling through all three at once?" I asked.

Torrence hesitated before saying.

"I do not crochet as much as I once did, but that is an apt comparison, yes."

Sol's mouth dropped open a bit, and Seamus snickered.

"You used to crochet?" she asked.

Torrence only smiled. I think. I mean, on a bull's face that could easily have been gas.

"I'm liking you more and more, Torrence," I added, before Torrence could take offense at Sol's question, or Seamus' laughter. I doubt either Sol or Seamus meant to offend—Sol hadn't sounded condescending at all, just surprised, and I think Seamus was more amused at Sol's surprise than the fact that Torrence crocheted. Seamus' Moms had shown me a quilt he'd made last summer, and he basically never stopped drawing, so I didn't think he found arts and crafts to be degrading activities.

"I spend more time in the community gardens now, but when I first moved to Unterberg I became quite an avid crocheter," said Torrence, without a trace of defensiveness in his voice.

There was definitely a smile on his face now. I mean ok, if I'd seen a bull on Earth doing that I would have assumed it was about to vomit or something, but knowing that the brain behind the bull face was in full control of its expressions, and that it functioned in a bipedal society where facial expressions were a thing, that had to be a smile.

"So, why does traveling through a pocket dimension tend to make most magic users, and especially shifters, nauseous?"

I was trying to bring us back to our original digression, even as I reminded myself that we were in a damned hurry, because, honestly, I needed a minute for my guts to realign themselves, and I would take any information I could get that I didn't have to wrestle out of people. It had been an uninformative few weeks and easy answers felt like a milkshake going down right about now.

"The theory is that shifters have a difficult time bringing both of their selves along, as their animal form is in its own dimensional pocket, so bringing both along for one of these trips requires leaps of physics that aren't particularly comfortable. As for most other magic users, no one is sure why it affects them adversely early on, but most of us grow used to it with practice."

"Interesting… I wonder how much of that is because most magic users probably have alternate forms they could reach for if they had the time and focus to access them. Maybe they get more comfortable with the shift as they grow more and more distant from their other forms." Trev had explained the bit about all magic users having access to alternate forms in an attempt to fill the awkward silence while we had waited at Rhelia's bedside after I'd felt well enough to get out of my own recovery bed. It may also have been his attempt to address our Mom's suggestion to "teach her everything." I won't pretend I didn't miss some of the content, because I was distracted by how distant Trev had felt ever since the whole accidentally-killing-his-mate incident, but the gist had been what I'd just explained; people were limited by their perceptions of how their own magic worked, not actually by their DNA.

The ensuing expression on Torrence's face made me think that cows must be really good at poker.

"I'm surprised that you've been exposed to that theory. You have only been aware of our world for a few weeks, no?" he asked.

I nodded.

"I'm getting a crash course, I guess you could say. So, does that mean you subscribe to the theory that all magic users can be shifters, and vice versa?" I asked.

When Trev had explained it, he'd made it sound as though that theory was not widely accepted in the magical community. Most folks still held with the idea that you only had access to whatever magic you had "inherited." Technically, they were right, it was just that when you looked back through every single ancestor you'd ever had, you really had just about the entirety of human (and magical) diversity to choose from. Thanks to the unique intersection of epigenetics and dark matter, all you had to do was focus long enough to unlock it. Apparently, when you ignored your pre-conceived notions and focused on what was actually in your DNA, you got… near infinite possibilities.

Still, not knowing how Torrence felt about that idea, I tried to put my own poker face in place. I wasn't sure how well I did. I probably just looked constipated.

Torrence tilted his head noncommittally, but said nothing.

Then a voice from somewhere beyond the foyer asked, "Torrence, are you going to bring our guests out of the entryway at any point this evening?"

The vaguely familiar voice set tiny warning bells jangling in my mind.

A moment later, a willow of a woman with yellow hair, long but elegantly pointed ears, and green skin barely visible underneath her off-white tunic and calfskin pants, walked through the hallway, stopping short of us by a few meters and wrinkling her nose in obvious disgust. Her violet eyes pulsed momentarily, and then we were all relieved of the smell of Sol's rejected meals. I glanced cautiously at the floor, and confirmed that the mess was gone.

That was when I first really took in our surroundings—aside from the shiny marble floor and the various bits of bull-person in front of me, that is. It was like my fear of taking too good a look at Sol's opening volley (which I was still un-comfortably close to copying) had given me a kind of tunnel vision that blocked out everything but the furry face in front of me.

Now, with the threat of witnessing someone else's lost meal removed, my vision opened up to encompass a marble hallway that featured some rather bland painted landscapes trussed up in heavily gilded frames, along with a mirror large enough to serve a small rugby squad who all wanted to check their teeth at the same time.

It was quite spacious and, despite the fact that it could easily have contained Sol's entire mountain cabin, it appeared to be only the foyer.

"Soledad, Seamus, Victoria, please come in," said the woman, who I now recognized as Nethia, the one who had given the impression she was in charge of the Unterberg council the last time we'd been here.

"Um… not that it's any of my business, but are you here just to talk to us, or is this your home too?"

"You're correct. It's none of your business."

I nodded.

"Fair. Only, if anything, it looks like you live here rather than Torrence. I mean, stale art, flashy mirrors, marble… a general sense of trying too hard," I continued, my tongue deciding that sass was appropriate even though Nethia could probably make me disappear from Unterberg with the sort of finality and discretion that it was generally unwise to provoke.

"Will you come in?" she asked again, ignoring my commentary.

I turned to look at Sol and Seamus, and caught Torrence rolling his eyes in a way that made me think that one of us was being ridiculous, but I wasn't sure who.

I looked at Sol, who, despite still being a bit off-color, looked like she was ready to bite Nethia for her condescending tone. I shook my head subtly. Pissing Nethia off verbally was one thing, sinking your teeth into her was another. We didn't need an incident. In fact, from what little Rhelia had told us in her communique, Torrence might be one of the few people who could help us, and our current situation suggested he was unlikely to do so without Nethia's say-so. When I turned and caught Seamus' eye, he was staring fixedly at Nethia with something like awe. Or it might have been fear, it was hard to tell.

"Look, we were in a bit of a hurry before we got sidetracked by Torrence here. We'd like to get back to what we were doing, but Torrence made it sound like some top-secret shit was about to go down, so… here we are. Want to tell us what the hell's going on?" I asked.

"That thing you're doing here," Torrence began, exchanging a glance with Nethia, "Would it happen to include searching for your dragon sister?"

I shrugged.

"My dragon sister?" I replied, deciding to play dumb. I wasn't feeling overly generous now that Nethia had shown up. After all, Seamus had warned us not to trust the green lady, a description that fit Nethia all too well. And our whole mission with Rhelia was entirely secret—so secret that we didn't even know exactly why she was in Unterberg—and I wasn't convinced these two needed to know any of it yet. Rhelia had mentioned Torrence was a contact, but she didn't say if he was someone she trusted.

"The dragon sister everyone else believes is dead," Nethia clarified.

"What makes you think that she isn't?" I asked.

"The fact that she's unconscious in the next room," Nethia replied.

And for some reason that was when Sol decided to shift to her panther form and launch herself at the willowy green woman's throat.

"**S**OL! ¡NO LA mates!"

It was the best I could do in the time it took for Sol to turn into 300 lbs of snarling black fury and pin Nethia to the golden-veined marble floor. Sol's jaws surrounded the all-too-delicate-looking green neck of the Unterberg council member, and for a moment I was certain that I was already too late, that the woman was dead, and that we were definitely going to Unterberg's prison for this, or worse.

Then I heard Nethia grunt.

"Get this blasted beast OFF of me!"

Sol growled, but didn't move, and Torrence and I stood frozen where we were.

Seamus was smiling, with his hands in his pockets, as though his friends habitually launched themselves at green-skinned, pointy-eared foreign dignitaries. Come to think of it, it was possible that they did. I didn't really know what Seamus' other friends were like, or how most werewolves interacted with other magical creatures.

Meanwhile, I only had one guess as to what had prompted Sol to act like a man-eating cat from a cheap horror flick, assuming it wasn't solely based on Seamus' warning about Nethia—which was a possibility—but this situation was too precarious to do anything but go with my gut.

"I think…" I began, even as I started edging my way towards the open archway that Nethia had been gesturing towards when she mentioned our unconscious friend, "…that I'm just going to go make sure that Rhelia is alright, while everyone else holds perfectly still."

Sol's tail flicked in an enthusiastic twitch that repeated three times, making me think that I was onto something, and Seamus nodded like I had the right idea.

"I really do suggest that you not move at all, Nethia, and I have a feeling the same goes for you, Torrence."

"Agreed," Torrence said quietly, as I passed through the archway into what looked like a large living room.

The room was furnished with daybeds, ornately carved to look like they were naturally occurring shrubberies that just happened to have soft cushions in them, and surrounded by walls full of more elaborate paintings in even more ornate frames, all circling a medium-sized raised koi pond covered with a plate of glass that turned it into a functional coffee table, with the added zing of some lazily circling koi fish.

On the daybed directly across from me (leaving the koi pond between us, and the other daybeds to the left and right of me) lay an unconscious Rhelia. For a moment, the sight made my breathing hitch. I was in no state of mind to see Rhelia lying inert, so soon after her feigned death, but, luckily, after only a heartbeat or two, I saw her chest rise and fall. The sight broke the hold of whatever had been keeping my lungs and limbs from moving, and I ran to Rhelia's side.

Her pulse was normal, her breathing even, and her ebon, iridescent skin looked the way it usually did. Aside from the fact that she didn't wake up when I touched her, or even when I shook her—

gently at first and then more vigorously—she seemed fine.

"She won't wake up," I half shouted across the room.

Sol's hearing was excellent in panther form, and Seamus had followed me as far as the entrance to the living area, but was still within view of Sol and her prey. I probably didn't need to yell, but tell that to my barely-not-panicked brain.

I heard a small yelp from Nethia's direction and then, "I can wake her if you get this infernal cat off of me."

That was followed by another yelp.

"I think you'll have to figure out a way to wake her now, Nethia. From under the 'infernal cat,' if you really want to keep your throat," I called back.

I hoped Sol wasn't drawing blood yet. I didn't want to go to Unterberg's prison, and I had no idea how Torrence would side in this thing if we wound up in front of the council again.

Then I heard a gasp at my side, and all thoughts of the council were forgotten.

Rhelia's eyes blinked open, and instantly narrowed at the archway across from us.

"Careful, Ssssol! She'ssss a Dragon Hunter!"

"S HE'S A WHATTY-what now?" I asked, before my brain caught up and reminded me that the name was fairly self-explanatory.

"Dragon Hunter. A group of people reviled by my own, assss you might imagine."

Rhelia had already gotten up and started crossing the room back to the ornate foyer, where Sol was hopefully not yet tearing out Nethia's throat, so I was following her even as I asked inane questions.

Seamus nodded, smiling, at Rhelia, and then stepped in behind me as I followed the irate weredragon into the foyer.

"That seems like a really dumb hobby," I supplied, as we walked through the archway and took in the tableau of Sol, still enveloping Nethia's throat with her teeth, while pinning her to the marble floor with the entirety of her 300 pounds of feline fury. In other words, right where I'd left her. Torrence, good as his word, hadn't moved an inch.

Nethia looked as though she'd tried to move at least once, but had eventually learned the error of her ways. There was now a disturbing amount of feline saliva, along with some ugly looking scrapes, visible just to the sides of Sol's jaws.

"That issss an undersssstatement, Living Cat."

Rhelia's use of my nickname caused some of the tension to leave my shoulders. As though her calling me something silly meant that maybe we weren't necessarily watching our mission completely unravel in front of us. After all, she was the only one who knew exactly what our mission was.

"So… dare I ask what kind of moron takes up Dragon Hunting?" I asked, glaring at Nethia in a way that I hoped conveyed my full disapproval.

"Thesssse two moronsss," Rhelia replied, gesturing in a way that encompassed both Nethia and Torrence. To be fair, that gesture encompassed Sol as well, but I thought it was safe to assume that was just positioning, and not because Sol was secretly a dragon killer.

"That's a lie!" Nethia shouted, or tried to shout, from between Sol's jaws. "The Dragon Hunters were never more than a myth," she said, with less force, thus sparing herself more scrapes from Sol's teeth.

"You rendered me unconscioussss assss ssssoon assss Torrencsssse told you I wassss inquiring about Dragon Hunterssss," Rhelia countered. "And your magic may not be assss ssssstrong assss you think it issss, becausssse I heard you asssssking Torrencsssse why he revealed the truth to me even assss I wassss losssssing consssscioussssnessss."

"Ugh, you can turn off the accent, dragonling, it tires me," Nethia grumbled from the floor.

"All the more reasssson to keep ussssing it, then."

"You can turn off the accent?" I asked, completely derailed from the more important topics at hand.

Rhelia just leveled a gaze at me that made it clear we were not talking about this right now.

"I believe we owe you an explanation," Torrence said, finally breaking the silence he'd kept since Sol had first pounced on Nethia.

"No shit," I replied, turning my gaze from Rhelia to him. "Better get started. I don't know how long Sol can hold her jaws open like that."

Sol growled and flicked her tail. I wasn't sure if she was agreeing with me, or objecting to the insult to her stamina. Either way, Torrence seemed to take it as his cue to get started.

"I think we would all be more comfortable in the living room," he hazarded, but Sol growled again at the suggestion, so he began talking even as Nethia whispered, "Torrence, don't."

"Nethia and I were both members of the elite Dragon Hunters. We each have our reasons for not wanting anyone to know of our past, not least of which is that we all took oaths of secrecy when the Dragon Hunters disbanded. Just talking to you now may render our lives forfeit, but the alternative is taking your lives, and that is something I will not do. Though you should know—what we tell you now may make you targets for whatever members of the Dragon Hunters remain."

Rhelia and I exchanged a glance with Seamus, and Sol flicked her tail from her place atop Nethia.

"Well, they can get in line," I sighed. I mean, it wasn't like it would matter, if we couldn't stop Rebecca Dryer from blowing up the entire world.

I looked at Rhelia again. "You think it likely they can help us?"

Rhelia shrugged, but her face was as hard as the stone her skin resembled.

"Unfortunately, I cannot think of anyone better suited to help find a missing cadre of dragons than those who used to make such their livelihood. It is why I came here. Though I admit that I did not expect to find out that Torrence and Nethia were Dragon Hunters themselves, I was merely hoping they could point me in the right direction."

I nodded, and worked very hard to swallow my comment about Rhelia's sibilant accent disappearing.

Torrence looked between us and then down to Nethia again.

"Soledad, if I can extract an oath from her not to harm you or your friends, will you release Nethia?" he asked.

Sol's tail flicked, in what I took to be an affirmative, and Torrence must have taken it as one too.

"Nethia, will you swear on your blood and mine not to harm these four individuals?"

Nethia glared at Torrence with such vehemence that I half expected him to burst into flames.

"Or do I need to bind you here and take them to my own apartments so that you cannot interfere?" he continued.

Nethia sighed, and then nodded. I wondered what "binding" actually meant, if it was bad enough to make Nethia concede, but at least my question about living arrangements had finally been answered.

"Your word, Nethia," Torrence prompted.

"I give you my word, Torrence."

Torrence just glared at Nethia for a long moment, then she took a deep breath and tried again.

"By your blood and mine, I give my oath that I will not harm Rhelia Wyvern, Soledad Sierra Oscura, Seamus Hunter, or Victoria Adelaide Marmot."

I felt a warm buzz in the air, while a smell like a desert thunderstorm permeated the room before fading suddenly.

In a blink, Sol was standing in front of us wearing a tight fitting pair of jeans and a soft cotton shirt. She looked down at herself and smiled.

"You're so useful, Gatita."

I smiled in return.

"I don't even try."

Rhelia looked between the two of us with something like exasperation before turning to the green-skinned elf now cradling her neck, and the poker-faced tauren standing next to her. If she'd been in her dragon form, I would have expected the two of them to be cinders in another heartbeat, but instead of fire, she seared them with words.

"Now that Soledad is no longer about to kill you, we have no more time for idle chatter. You will help us, or we will reveal your past to the Unterberg council as well as the Elder Dragons. I don't have to remind you what that will do to your lives as you know them. You will lead us to the missing dragons right now, or you will die horribly by the hands of those who owe you justice."

THE ROOM THAT we stood in was dimly lit and heavily warded—at least, that's what I assumed was making it feel like a contained thunderstorm was right on top of our heads even though the circular space was entirely indoors, and not large enough to contain any actual weather events. That didn't stop the air from smelling like salt and ozone.

As I took in the flickering torches that lit the dark stone walls, I mused at how my actual magical knowledge was severely limited, but the fact that I'd read a lot of fantasy books and played a fair few role playing games somehow had trained my brain to interpret the feeling as indicating the presence of wards. I'd made a few gut decisions based on my fictional expertise in the last few weeks, and so far they'd all paid off. So much so that I was starting think that all of the nights I'd stayed up playing WoW or reading fantasy books instead of doing homework weren't the waste I had originally suspected them of being.

Anyway, aside from a giant salt circle etched out around the room, encompassing all of us standing within it, and the intense non-weather-related pressure that filled the space, this room could have easily been someone's sunroom. That is, it could have if any of the walls had been windows instead of heavy-looking, unpolished black marble. As it was, it felt more like a tomb.

Five of us stood on the points of a star while Nethia stood in the center of the whole thing. Rhelia stood at the top point, facing the center, and I stood to her right, while Sol stood to her left and Seamus stood to my right, with Torrence standing to his left on the final point of the star. It was extremely tempting to ask Sol to switch to her panther form so I could start making Sabrina jokes, but I restrained myself. Barely.

The urge to break the tension that had been mounting since we'd left Nethia's apartment in Unterberg was strong, bad jokes aside. After Rhelia had made it clear that Nethia and Torrence had no choice but to help us, Nethia had said little beyond explaining that if we wanted their help she would need to conduct a blood ritual (whatever that meant) in whichever realm we suspected the missing weredragons were being held. Which had meant a really awkward trip through the shadowed streets of Unterberg as we made our way to a seam that led to Earth, and then another stomach-churning teleport thanks to Torrence. This time, Seamus threw up. Sol probably had nothing left, and I had decided that I was just going to accept that multiple "me"s needed to make it through the trip and try to relax into it. Weirdly, that seemed to have worked, and I didn't feel nearly as sick this time as I had the trip before. I didn't bother to question why my own method of shifting through time and space didn't seem to make anyone sick, but filed it away to ponder another day.

Meanwhile, once we'd all finished being ill, or barely ill, or barely not ill, depending on who we were talking about, Nethia led us deeper and deeper into what appeared to be a subterranean lair, judging by the earthy smell, the lack of natural light, and the stagnant air that filled the passage-ways. Torrence had teleported us directly in-side the wherever we were, so we had no points of ref-erence for where we might be in the world, which I guessed was on purpose.

Certainly, if I'd had Rhelia glaring at me with the degree of hatred she was leveling at Torrence and Nethia right now, I wouldn't want her to be able to find me later either.

"So, if you despise Dragon Hunters so much, why are we here?" I had whispered to her, as we'd all filed down a long earthen corridor behind Nethia and Torrence.

"These people slaughtered my people in droves, for centuries, allegedly in service to MOME's crusade against us, but in reality simply for the coin they were paid. They were mercenaries who took hundreds of missions against any creature too difficult for MOME's own elite squads, but they specialized in destroying us at any cost. I would as soon wipe them from the face of the realms as work with them."

I stared at Rhelia, wondering if she even realized that she hadn't answered my question, or that she was still speaking without her sibilant accent.

Then she turned to me and sighed.

"But there will be no realms left, if we do not find my brethren quickly. We have used every trick that we can think of, and none have worked. My people like to pretend that the Dragon Hunters are as much a myth as most believe them to be. It is better for us if no one believes they exist, but we know better. They found us, unerringly, whenever we wandered outside of our own realm during the Dragon Genocide. If anyone can find Siara and the others, the Dragon Hunters can."

After a moment of silence, I finally asked a question—the question that was ringing loudest in my brain.

"Ok. I have a feeling this was mentioned in my dragon orientation, but… what was the Dragon Genocide, exactly?"

Rhelia stopped to stare at me for a moment before resuming her stride and pulling me along with her through the stone corridor.

"It was MOME's attempt to kill us all. They claimed it was because we were too dangerous, too difficult to hide from the non-magical humans. But really, it was just that they were frightened of us."

"So they tried to wipe you all out? If they were afraid of you, why would they do something likely to start a war with you?"

"That was precisely it. They could not risk a war with us. We are too powerful for a full-scale assault. Instead they sent assassins after us, and only when we left the safety of our own realm. We did not know who was responsible, at first. We were not even sure the attacks were connected, for a long time.

"But later, centuries after it began, we captured some MOME operatives who knew what was going on, and discovered the truth. The cowards never even came after us themselves, merely spread anti-dragon propaganda—attempting to set the rest of the magical world against us—and then sent Dragon Hunters after us whenever we stood in any realm but our own."

The way her mouth had formed the words "Dragon Hunters" made it look like she was about to be ill, but she clearly held a grudging respect for their ability to track down dragons. And I had to agree with the reasoning that had brought us here. We were out of time and options. If there was a shortcut to finding Siara, we had to take it, even if it was risky as hell and involved a centuries-old enemy.

Which is why we had all blithely followed two people we barely knew into the bowels of Gwen-knew-where, so that we could trust one of them with something called a blood ritual that was supposed to tell us exactly where the weredragons that shared Rhelia's blood were being held.

From the looks on everyone's faces when Nethia had said there would be a blood ritual, that shit was a big magical no-no. No one had explained why yet, so I just filed it away with the three thousand

and one other things I didn't understand, but would have to ask about later when we weren't fighting the clock.

And here we were.

I looked around the circle again, and vaguely wondered what we would have done if Seamus hadn't been here. Did we have to have a person on each of the five points of the star, along with someone in the middle, or could Nethia have completed the spell from one of the points? Did any of us need to be there besides Nethia and Rhelia? Or would this whole thing be impossible if Seamus hadn't shown up? I fought off the shudder that precognition triggered in me, because Seamus couldn't help seeing the future, and everything he'd told me about it so far made me think he hated it.

When I heard the sound of metal singing through air, my head whipped up just in time to see Seamus leap in front of a blade that had clearly been heading directly for Torrence. I almost screamed, as I thought it had hit Seamus in the center of his chest, but he'd leapt with his arms crossed in front of him, and I was suddenly, desperately glad for his abilities as a seer. Nethia was already pinned under the giant panther that was Soledad, and Rhelia had drawn two daggers from somewhere, placing one at Nethia's throat, somewhat redundantly. I didn't really notice how any of that had happened, because my body was too busy moving me to Seamus' side.

The dagger that Nethia had thrown had impaled his forearm, and it looked like it had pinned it to his chest, but not deeply enough to pierce any vital organs, I thought.

"Rhelia, we're going to need you over here," I said, noting the unnatural pallor of Seamus' face. It was a serious wound no matter what, but I didn't like the sweat that was beading on his forehead already.

There were sounds of movement behind me, but I couldn't tell what was going on, and didn't turn to find out.

"Seamus?" I asked, as his eyes started to close. "Seamus!"

"Allow me to help, Victoria," said Torrence.

"Why would I trust you to help? Your friend just tried to kill him!"

"She was trying to kill me, I believe."

Right. Seamus had been jumping in front of Torrence to save his life. Why would he do that?

"Seamus? Why?" I asked, not letting him go.

"I have some healing ability, Victoria, and I believe Nethia's daggers are poisoned. Seconds matter."

"Rhelia!" I shouted. Rhelia was supposed to be one of the best healers in all the realms, and I would be damned if I let a Dragon Hunter "heal" my friend/boyfriend, whatever Seamus was.

There were more sounds behind me, grunts and thuds, and metal scraping stone.

"Living Cat, let the cow heal him. He is bound by blood," she called, her voice not getting any closer.

I looked at Seamus' face, tight with pain, and then leveled my gaze at Torrence, who, I was surprised to see, was looking at Seamus with tears in his eyes.

"If he dies, Torrence, I swear to everything that I hold dear, I will make you wish it had been you instead," I hissed, before letting go of Seamus gently and allowing Torrence to collect him in his arms from his place on the floor behind him.

"Believe me, Victoria, I already wish that it had been."

LUCKILY, TORRENCE WAS not trying to kill Seamus. Indeed, in a few short minutes, Seamus was no longer sweating, overly pale, or bleeding. By then Rhelia was approaching and I finally looked over at what she and Sol had been up to, which apparently was trussing Nethia up like a holiday hog, even though she appeared to be unconscious.

"Is she dead?" I asked, glancing at her still form again.

"I am not certain," said Rhelia. "But we did not kill her, if that is what you are asking."

I looked at Rhelia, then over to Sol, who was also coming over to check on Seamus.

I pulled farther away to make space for Rhelia. I hoped she would confer with Torrence about Seamus' healing.

"How can you not be sure if she's dead?" I asked Sol, since Rhelia was busy.

Sol looked over at Nethia and frowned.

"I don't know. Before I could reach her she collapsed and her eyes rolled into the back of her head. I think she still has a pulse, but... it's not strong."

To my surprise, it was Torrence who spoke next. He stood up from where he'd been tending Seamus, leaving him in Rhelia's care to come stand beside us and look at the green-skinned woman who'd just tried to kill him.

"It is the oath," he said, after a moment. "She was likely trying to kill me so that she would be free of it. She swore on both of our blood, and the only way to be free of an oath like that is for one of us to die. However, when Seamus jumped in front of the blade, she broke her word instead, so the blood oath took her. There may not be anything left of her now."

"Fuck," I muttered, looking at Nethia again. "What about the spell she was going to cast?"

Torrence took a deep breath.

"I can cast it, though it will not be as strong."

"What does that mean?" I asked.

"It should serve us well enough, but it won't last very long or be portable. If Nethia had cast it, we could have tied it to an object, a weapon, a jewel, whatever you like, and it could have led any of you on your search. The version I know… well, I cannot tie it to anything but myself. I'm afraid you'll be stuck with me until you find your weredragons."

"Considering the fact that we have less than 40 hours to find them, I think I can live with that."

I looked over to Rhelia, assuming that she was going to be less than pleased at this turn of events, but she was too caught up in whatever she was doing to Seamus to have noticed. Either that, or she didn't care.

Not having anything else to do, I looked around the room, and my eyes inevitably fell to where Nethia lay at Sol's feet once more.

"Not that I'm objecting or anything, but… if Nethia is as good as dead, why did you bother to truss her up like that?" I asked.

I almost jumped when Rhelia's ice-cold voice replied, "So that she can pay for her crimes against the Dragon Realm."

When I turned to look at her, she was standing, supporting a groggy but mostly-conscious Seamus, and faint wisps of smoke were twining up from her mouth.

UNFORTUNATELY, RHELIA'S RAGE was going to have to wait a hot minute, because we had to start the whole damned spell-casting thing over again.

"What does the pentagram actually do?" I asked, as we scattered salt in the same pattern on the black marble floor that it had formed just before Nethia caused a scene by trying to kill people.

There was a moment of silence before I looked pointedly at Torrence and he answered.

"Sorry, I did not think you were asking me. I am not generally the magic casting expert in any given crowd. I forgot that you are all shifters. As you've no doubt guessed, a pentagram is not required for mages to access their magic."

I snorted at that, since, yeah… not a single person of the magical persuasion who had tried to kill me in the past few weeks had bothered to draw any-thing on the ground in salt first.

"But," continued Torrence patiently, "the magic that Dragon Hunters use for tracking is… despised. It is also easily noticed, and tracked, if it is cast out in the open. Hence, we are here in a heavily warded chamber, and casting it in the middle of a pentagram. Blood magic and demon summoning are the primary reasons you would use a pentagram. Otherwise, they can help if you are afraid of harming those around you with unwieldy magic. They act as containment for spell work."

"So, beginners, blood mages, and warlocks, got it."

Torrence looked up from where he was pouring salt onto the floor and raised a bovine brow.

"Indeed, that sums it up nicely."

"Warlocks?" asked Seamus from where he was leaning up against the wall.

"Anyone who summons demons for magical pur-poses," Sol clarified.

"Why else would someone summon a demon?" Seamus asked.

"Well, now that I've met Azrael, I could think of a couple reasons," I muttered.

Sol chuckled, and Seamus' cheeks reddened.

"For anyone with their own dark matter, sex with a succubus would still qualify as magical purposes. It amplifies power," Torrence explained. "Now, if a non-magical person summoned a demon in order to have sex, that might qualify as non-magical purposes."

"How would a non-magical person summon a demon?" Seamus and I asked, at the same time.

"You only need a demon's name to summon them," Torrence replied mildly, as he finished the circle on the floor. "Keeping the demon from killing you for interrupting its nap, on the other hand, might require a fair amount of magic. Succubi are often the exception to that rule, if you're polite in your requests, since they benefit from being invited to feed."

Then Torrence took a deep breath and turned towards Rhelia, who had been staring broodingly at Nethia's unconscious form, where it lay on the floor outside of our newly recast circle.

"I'm ready to begin, if you are," he said.

Rhelia shook her head, as if clearing her thoughts, and turned towards Torrence. Her golden eyes still burned with something like hatred, but whether it was for Nethia, for Torrence, or for what she was about to do, I wasn't sure. Perhaps all of the above.

"Assss ready assss I'll ever be."

I wondered what it meant that her sibilant accent was back.

"I will do my best to make it painless," Torrence said, stretching out his fur-covered, but otherwise human-looking hand.

"You know it issss not the pain that botherssss me, Hunter," she replied.

The way she said "Hunter" made it sound like the basest insult, but Torrence didn't even flinch. I was having a very difficult time sorting out what made him tick.

As he took Rhelia's hand. though, I heard him offer the barest explanation.

"I have not performed this ritual for centuries. I abandoned my position in the Hunters when I finally realized that, despite all of MOME's propaganda, your people were as innocent as any other, and more so than many. It does not excuse what I've done, and I will willingly go with you to face the punishment of the Dragon Elders once we have found those you seek, but I wish you to know that I do not lightly take on the burden of blood magic once more."

And then he slashed open her palm with a dagger.

Rhelia had clearly been expecting it, even if I hadn't, and barely winced at the pain.

To my surprise, she also did not stab him repeatedly or take on her dragon form and incinerate his head, which was kind of what her facial expressions had been telegraphing ever since I'd woken her up on Nethia's couch.

Before I could even come up with something to say (sorry, you're bleeding, do you need a bandage or anything?) Torrence cut an identical slash into his own palm. Then, slightly more hygienically than I'd expected, given how this whole thing had started, he gently tipped Rhelia's palm until the blood that had been pooling there ran into the open wound in his hand.

Torrence grimaced, and Rhelia's eyes flared in the low light of the stone room.

"If you usssse thissss for any purposssse but the one we've requesssssted, I will end you sssso painfully you will wish you had never exissssted."

Torrence nodded, but said nothing, his eyes drifting shut in apparent effort and concentration.

The rest of us just stood there awkwardly for a few minutes, while he did his secret blood magic thing.

Is this going to take a while? I asked Rhelia eventually.

Did you have ssssomewhere better to be, Living Cat?

Nope. Just have to pee.

Rhelia's eyes flashed again, but this time I thought it was with contained amusement. Good, that's what I'd been hoping for.

I have never sssseen a blood ritual performed before. It issss a forbidden art in both the dragon realm and the human one.

Is that just because it's super creepy, or…?

It issss consssssidered a violation. From my undersssstanding it requiressss the casssster to project their own dark matter into the blood of another. Thissss issss almosssst alwayssss againsssst the other'ssss will.

And how does that help us?

It can be ussssed to track people. I share sssssome of my blood with Ssssiara, and thussss my blood, in the right handssss, can be ussssed to find her. It issss how the Dragon Hunterssss tracked ussss and alssssso how they bound ussss. It issss the only way they were ever able to defeat ussss. Or ssssso the sssstoriessss ssssay.

Let me guess, the dragons did whatever they could to make sure those stories didn't get around.

We had little to do that the Dragon Hunterssss themsssselvessss did not do for ussss. They had cornered the market, if you will.

The thought of Torrence and his allies using the dragons' own blood against them made my stomach turn. Especially when I considered that if I'd been born a few hundred years earlier I certainly would have made the list of acceptable targets. The thought hit me a little bit harder than it should have. I still hadn't fully wrapped my brain around the idea of being a dragon.

Finally, Torrence's eyes opened, and his hand glowed a dull red.

"I believe this will work. As I said, it would be much stronger if Nethia had cast it—she was our expert blood mage—but this will suffice to let me lead you, as long as we are quick. I am sorry that I could not attach it to some sort of talisman, and thus free you of the burden of my company."

Rhelia rolled her eyes, and the rest of us just stared at each other in bewilderment.

"I'm hungry," Seamus said from the floor. "Is anyone else hungry?"

~~~
~~~

We arrived in the Dragon Realm a few moments later.

In a display that seemed to fit no one's mood, the moon was full and shining in a cloudless, star-filled sky, as we stepped out into the same valley where we'd arrived the very first time Rhelia had brought us here. I took a deep breath, filled with the scent of earth and wildflowers, and then almost choked on my own saliva when I saw Torrence basically prance through the aforementioned wildflowers and then fling himself down on the ground to stare at the sky.

Ok. Maybe the clear sky and moonlight fit someone's mood.

Rhelia was looking at the bull-man as if he had two bovine heads instead of one, and I almost lost my shit at her expression.

"I think he likes flowers," I offered.

Rhelia turned her baffled gaze to me, then rubbed her eyes.

"Can you pleasssse take Nethia to your brother to deal with, and collect whoever issss available to help ussss?" she asked. "We do not have time for all of ussss to walk there, and you should ssssave your shiftssss with multiple people for when it countssss."

"Sure," I said, grabbing the still-unconscious Nethia by the arm, and picturing Rhelia's home in the small main drag that constituted the were-dragon portion of the Dragon Realm. "Does Trev know a good dungeon to throw her in?"

Rhelia's smile was cold, and didn't reach her eyes.

"More or lessss."

I decided I didn't really want to know, so I left Rhelia, Seamus, and Sol to keep Torrence in line. Or in flowers. Whatevs.

We'd debated rendering Torrence unconscious for the duration of our visit to the Dragon Realm, and Torrence hadn't objected, but he'd admitted that he couldn't be sure that the spell would hold up if we had to knock him out and revive him. He seemed to sympathize completely with Rhelia's reluctance to take a known Dragon Hunter into the Dragon Realm—one that she wasn't planning to throw into prison immediately, that is, she'd been more than happy to bring Nethia along—but we couldn't figure out any way to avoid bringing Torrence along, awake, without devoting way too much time and energy to what was likely to just be a quick respite on our way to a very difficult rescue mission. We had to come to the Dragon Realm to drop off Nethia, debrief Trev, and see if we could recruit a few more people for the next part of our plan. Not knowing how much MOME knew about our movements, and not being sure when they were planning their own attack against the non-magical world, we couldn't afford to waste time keeping Torrence away from the Dragon Realm right now. I needed to minimize my shifting so I would have enough energy for our rescue operation, and any other iteration of the plan split the group in too many ways to make sense. In other words, we were stuck with him. But that didn't mean that Rhelia wanted to drag him into the middle of the residential portion of the Dragon Realm. So, we'd decided the most efficient thing for conserving my energy and keeping Torrence as much in the dark as possible was for me to do in-world shifts only, to avoid shifting between realms, and to take as few people with me as possible for each shift. Hence why I was leaving everyone in this field of wildflowers out of sight of town, while I took Nethia off to be delivered to justice.

Nethia, or her barely living body, and I arrived directly in front of the door to Rhelia's office, skipping past trivialities like front doors and the rest of the house, and I knocked before pushing it open to find Trevor staring intently at one of his two enormous monitors (not to be confused with Rhelia's even larger set of monitors, which took up the other half leg of the giant L desk covering half the walls), scanning through lines of code.

"Vic!" he said, sounding surprised to see me, even though I was pretty sure Rhelia had been communicating with him telepathically as soon as we'd hit Dragon Realm soil. I hadn't tried to get in touch because I'd been too wary of a cold reception.

"Hey," I said, wrapping him in a hug when he stood up to greet me. "I'm playing Hermes today. You've won a mostly dead Dragon Hunter, and a request for all the backup you can spare for a covert rescue operation."

Trev hugged me back with enough enthusiasm to erase some of the distance I'd felt between us in the past 48 hours, and then he looked at Nethia behind me (I'd left her in the doorway) and sighed.

"I'll have the Dragon Elders come collect her. Best if we don't let General Aira know she's here just yet," he said.

I didn't particularly want to know what they were going to do with her, or why General Aira should be kept in the dark, so I didn't ask. I just reminded myself that she'd tried to kill Torrence, almost killed Seamus instead, and had likely been trying to take out Torrence in order to kill ALL of us, so…

whatever they were going to do with her was fine with me.

"And my backup?" I asked.

"We don't have much we can spare from the twelve reconnaissance ops that General Aira is running. She's not willing to sit around and wait while we find Siara and Emil. Not to mention, she's unwilling to send any more big booms into MOME territory."

I raised an eyebrow for a moment, then my brain caught up.

"Right. No dragons or weredragons for this mission."

Trev nodded.

"In fact, Rhelia is probably going to be pissed at me, but…"

Trev's voice faded, and I wondered if he didn't want me to know that he was about to tell Rhelia she couldn't go, even though that had been obvious as soon as he'd mentioned the no weredragon thing. I assumed the only reason I was allowed to go was that I was just a baby weredragon, and a baby everything else, and… well, we needed my emergency escape powers. I was just about to ask Trev if the cat had his tongue, when that train of thought was derailed entirely by the sound of feathers brushing wood.

"Hullo, Luv," said a familiar voice behind me.

I turned to see a dark figure with silver wings blocking out most of the door frame, just as Trev said, "I suppose I can spare Azrael, though."

"WHAT IS SHE doing here?" Torrence asked, in a voice somewhere between turned on and put out. He was no longer lying in the meadow flowers gazing at the night sky. Instead he was standing in the meadow flowers, swaying gently, as though he were a flower himself and the wind had taken him. Somehow, he'd found time to make a crown of daisies and drape it be-tween his horns in the few minutes I'd been gone.

I tried staring into the moon to keep myself from laughing unnecessarily. I really didn't want to discourage anyone embracing nature, and it was honestly awesome that a giant bull-person like Torrence was super into flowers, but some visuals are just too striking to do anything but conjure mirth.

"Azrael was invited, because Azrael is part of our strike team," I replied, doing my best to gesture towards the succubus without looking directly at them again. Though it might have been an excellent way to avoid laughing at Torrence, I wasn't in the mood to be distracted by my own hormones, and Azrael was nothing if not distracting, when they weren't a demon squirrel.

Seamus, Sol, Torrence, and even Rhelia all took a moment to stare at Az, which made me work all the harder not to. Trevor stepped out from behind the succubus and made his way to Rhelia to wrap his arms around her, a gesture she returned in full as soon as she pulled her eyes away from Az. It didn't seem possessive at all; Trev had spent the whole day worried about her, and it showed.

"Please try to focus, people," I said, wanting to shove Azrael behind me or something. Not that it would have helped. They were a foot taller than I was. Maybe if I'd had a blanket or something, I could have done something effective, but as it was we were just going to have to push on through.

"Not even going to look at me, Vic?" Azrael's voice asked from behind my neck, apparently having closed the distance between us while I wasn't looking.

"You give me a headache," I replied, looking resolutely forward.

"I can fix that," Azrael said, running their breath along my shoulder in a way that left little confusion about how they would fix it.

"Yeah, maybe, but we don't have time for that, and I don't trust you not to steal my soul."

"Ugh, so tetchy."

"What do you mean she gives you a headache?" Torrence asked, seeming genuinely curious.

I normally would have insisted it was none of his damned business, but since I wanted to focus on anything other than the breath running over my shoulder, I threw a light elbow behind me and stepped forward without looking back, taking no small amount of pleasure in Az's muttered "ow, not nice."

"Azrael gives me a headache because I can see both of their forms at the same time, unless we're surrounded by people who all find the same form attractive."

"Interesting," said Torrence, looking me up and down in a way that made me wonder what assumptions he'd made about me, and how he was rearranging them.

I shook my head, reminding myself that I didn't really care what the giant tauren thought of my sexual orientation, and hoping to get us all back on target. Azrael had a way of making everyone in the immediate area unnaturally horny and that was actually the larger portion of why I wasn't looking at them.

It was true that it gave me a bit of a headache to see a six foot tall, gorgeous man with giant silver wings superimposed on top of a six foot tall gorgeous woman with giant silver wings, both of whom were largely naked and who moved at exactly the same time and said the same things. But more than that, I found both of them incredibly hot, and it was distracting, obnoxious, and felt really awkward because part of my brain still recognized Azrael as a red-skinned, largely furless, demon-squirrel thing.

"So, about this mission," I tried to get everyone's attention, which had once more wandered back to Azrael. Trev was staring too now, his pupils wider than normal and his hand clenching Rhelia's even tighter than before.

"Damn it, Az, can't you put on more clothes or something!?"

"She's wearing a suit," Seamus said, still sounding awed.

"Really?" I almost turned around to check, but stopped myself just in time.

"Didn't want to be a distraction," Az said.

"Right. Thanks, I guess. So, then why…"

"Well, I'm still me, Luv. Can't turn that off."

I chuckled. "Not on this planet."

I felt fingers pinch my side, hard, and I shot another elbow behind me, this time without holding back at all, but the elbow connected with nothing but air and then, suddenly, Azrael was standing directly in front of me. Both of them.

The pinstripe suit that both forms were wearing just made the headache worse. The two outlines of the feminine and masculine atop each other were extra dizzying with the added barcode of the stripes.

"Can you just choose one?" I asked.

"Can you?" they replied.

"Touché."

I blinked and held the sides of my head.

"Seriously, does no one else have to put up with this?" I muttered.

Rhelia chuckled. "Once you said that you could see both, I started seeing the female form, but for me it flips all the way from one to the other."

I decided to close my eyes.

Azrael sighed dramatically.

"Alright, I will spare you. Vic, give Seamus a kiss."

I tried to glare at them with my eyes closed.

"I promise it'll help," Azrael said.

I opened my eyes and turned towards Seamus, who looked perfectly happy to oblige, and even did me the favor of nodding visibly, so I didn't have to ask.

Not wanting to drag this out any longer, I stepped over to Seamus, wrapped my arms around his waist and planted a kiss on his mouth. It was quick, and fairly chaste, since we were surrounded by people and about to head out on a potentially lethal rescue mission, but it was enough to wake up the mating bond within me and get my blood going. I stepped back quickly, before the mating bond could get too excited about anything, and looked around the field.

My eyes were instantly drawn to Azrael, who was now very decidedly a man wearing a pinstriped suit with no wings, silver or otherwise, in sight.

"Weird. You did mention once that my attraction varying could change how I saw you, but I didn't really believe you."

Azrael shrugged.

"I meant what I said. If you ever need to stop seeing double, try pushing your attraction more to one side or the other."

"But what if no one else is around?" I asked, before I could stop and think.

"Well, if no one is around, I'd prefer you were focused on me, Luv," Azrael said, with a grin that did strange things to my insides.

"If you weren't so damned good at killing vampires, you would be off the team right now."

"Oh, is that why the succubus is here?" Torrence said. "I had wondered."

"Doesn't everyone know that succubi are renowned vampire hunters?" I asked, looking from Sol to Rhelia, to Seamus, to Trev, to Torrence.

Judging by the blank stares I was getting, I was gonna have to go with "no."

"Huh, I just assumed that would be common knowledge. I mean, since when do I know anything about this world that you guys don't?" I shook my head. "Ok. So, we have our vampire take-out 'squad,' we have our intel, we have our hackers, we have our muscle and we have…"

"Our bait?" Seamus suggested, with a small frown.

"I was going to say decoy, but yeah. We have our bait."

In truth, the lines of our team weren't nearly that clear cut. Except for Seamus—he really was our bait.

"Now, can we please talk about the freaking plan? We're down to just over 36 hours before Rebecca Dryer makes good on her threat."

Everyone nodded and I took a deep breath, about to go over the details that Rhelia, Sol, Seamus, and I had sketched out as we'd made our way out of Nethia's underground spellcasting lair.

"Perhaps I can be of some use?" asked a familiar voice that had me spinning on my heel before I could even begin to speak. Of course she arrived from an angle that left her backlit by the sun—it wouldn't be dramatic enough otherwise—but eventually I made out a curvy silhouette, which was making its way closer and closer to our little posse.

"Hey Gwen," I said, sighing as the redheaded goddess of fortune came into full view. "I have a feeling you could be useful, yeah."

"**B**ECAUSE WE CAN'T risk them using you as a bomb," Trev said for what seemed like perhaps the 20th time.

I stared at the blue sky, took a deep breath of sun-warmed flowers, and wished that I'd walked off with the rest of the group when this argument had started. For some damned reason I'd wanted to show solidarity with my so-recently-estranged brother. Now I was wishing I'd just let him dig his own grave.

"They were more than happy to use you as one, Trevor! They could use any of us!" Rhelia's sibilant accent had dropped away for this argument, and I couldn't tell if that was because she was angry, or just impatient and the extra sibilance took too long. Maybe a bit of both.

"But dragons make the biggest bang," Trev replied. "Rhelia, we've been over this. MOME must have wanted to start small, or maybe Dryer was just in a hurry to get rid of me because of how much I know about MOME's inner workings, but you are made of much more dark matter than I am. You know that."

"And what of your sister? Victoria is a dragon and more, Trevor. How can you risk her becoming a weapon if you cannot risk me?"

"Vic has an emergency escape method that none of the rest of us do. She's probably the least likely to be captured of all of us," Trev said. His voice sounded firm, but I could tell Rhelia was wearing him down. "Vic, help me out here."

I stared at him for a moment, though my gaze had nothing on Rhelia's glare.

"Why on Earth, or any realm, would I help you keep a grown-assed woman from going on a mission she wants to be on? Especially when that woman spends half her time as a walking, flying, fire-breathing tank?"

"Because they could try to use her to destroy everyone?"

"How is that different from what they could do with any of us?" I asked.

"It's damage control," Trev insisted. "It's trying to make sure that the fewest people—"

"It's you being overprotective because you thought she was dead three days ago," I said, not willing to listen to the excuses anymore.

Rhelia actually laughed as all the fight went out of Trev in that moment, and then she was hugging him, and he was crying a bit, and then I thought I heard kissing, and that was lovely, but I didn't need to watch it, so I headed over to the huddle of all the sensible people who'd left that argument as soon as it started.

"You finally realized there was no way to win there?" Sol asked, as I wandered over to the group. Azrael and Gwen stood facing me already, but Sol and Seamus had both turned to see me as I approached.

I sighed.

"My brother probably hates me now," I muttered.

"Ah, so you stood for the side of reason?" Azrael asked.

"If Rhelia gets so much as a scratch on this mission, Trev's gonna blame me, personally."

"Ha! Only if he wants Rhelia to take his head off," Sol chuckled. "I can understand the reaction based on recent events, but if your brother is always that protective, Rhelia is going to find someone else to be her partner, 'mate' or no."

I sighed.

"I don't think he's that much of an idiot, but I haven't spent that much time with him in the last decade, so…" I shrugged.

Seamus tentatively wrapped one arm around my shoulders, and I leaned into him and wrapped my arms around his waist to let him know the touch was welcome.

"Don't ever let me be that much of an ass, ok?" I pleaded.

"You mean like earlier today when you tried to tell me I should go home?" Seamus asked.

I was reassured by the fact that he didn't let go of me, but it was a painful reminder of my own crappy reaction earlier.

"I'm sorry about that. I get nervous sometimes, about how little training you've had in combat. That's no excuse, though. You're as much of an adult as I am, and you can put yourself at risk as you see fit. Plus I need to remember that you have a much better idea of what risks lie ahead than most people." I almost kicked myself for that last part, not knowing how much of his abilities Seamus wanted the rest of our group to know about.

Seamus ignored the reference to his abilities as a seer, though, and kissed the top of my head in what would have been a patronizing way if I hadn't so richly deserved it.

"Lucky for you I was raised by wolves and have been conditioned to see protectiveness in all family and friends as a sign of affection."

I laughed then, thinking of all the wolves I'd known in my summers volunteering at the wildlife rescue. Seamus was spot on, they were all inherently protective of their pack.

A cough sounded behind us, causing half of us to turn around and the other half to look up. Seamus and I both turned at the same time, dropping our hold on one another, because the cough was directly behind us.

"I am going to sssstay behind and ssssift through ssssecurity feedssss from here, assss well assss run some additional code that might be helpful later," Rhelia said calmly, her arm wrapped around Trev's shoulders in almost the same way Seamus' had been wrapped around my own moments ago.

A few of us raised our eyebrows at that.

"And I am going to apologize profusely for being an overprotective git, and then be the one to patch Rhelia into the computers at MOME in order to let her run everything from her apartment on

Earth," Trev said, sounding more than a little sheepish.

"How is it that you are apologizing and also getting your way?" I asked, when no one else seemed inclined to question this.

To my satisfaction, it was Rhelia who answered.

"Becausssse, while I may be a better hacker, Trev issss more familiar with MOME'ssss protocolssss and he will be able to quickly insssstall a proxsssy devicssse that will allow me to monitor the necsssesssary ssssecurity feedssss. And I am better equipped to ssssearch for two weredragonssss than he issss. In addition, Trev has promissssed me that he will not interfere when I absssssolutely demolish MOME oncsssse we have gotten all of our people out."

I swallowed, because I didn't think Rhelia was joking, and I hadn't known that was on the "to-do" list for today.

"Do not worry, Living Cat. We have people behind MOME'ssss wallssss other than the prisonersss you will ressssscue now. Today issss not the day that MOME will burn."

I glanced at Seamus, saw him shudder, and wondered if he was just reacting to the violent glint in Rhelia's yellow eyes, or if he had seen something.

"We should go."

It was the first time Gwen had spoken since I'd walked over from Trev and Rhelia's argument, and I'd almost forgotten she was still here. I had half expected her to simply disappear while we were all distracted. It wouldn't have been the first time.

When we all looked at her expectantly, she just stared back for a moment.

"Oh fine. I suppose I can give you a lift," she muttered, before corralling us into a group hug and blinking us out of existence.

THE WHOLE THING about gods of serendipity is that they're really good for short cuts. Apparently, the way the tracking spell that Torrence had cast worked was that it more or less turned him into a walking compass—a compass for which magnetic north was always Siara. So, while our original plan had been to head to Earth via the seam in the dragon realm and then have me shift us in the general direction Torrence's compass pulled, Gwen showing up cut what might have been a longish game of Marco Polo down to two jumps. We first touched down in a nondescript alley in La Paz (blissfully devoid of human fluids, this time) with the idea that we should start with the last place we were certain MOME had held Siara and Emil. In addition, it was where Rhelia's Earth apartment was—a fact that had some of us raising eyebrows, since we hadn't known she'd had a place here until just before we'd left and Gwen asked us where we'd like to head first.

After Rhelia left us, a quick consult with Torrence and his Siara compass had us aiming NNW, and then in a single blink through space and time we were in front of a large, nondescript concrete building in downtown Phoenix, standing on a brightly lit piece of sidewalk that was still baking with the day's heat despite a darkened sky, the gathering clouds in the distance, and a wind that carried the scent of impending rain.

The good news was that I was fairly certain that we were standing in front of the same place where they'd held Seamus and me back when we were awaiting my sham of a trial, and that meant this wasn't just some random stop on the way to Siara and Emil, but rather was quite likely where they were being held. A quick look at Torrence confirmed it. He nodded and pointed inside the building.

"They are inside and down, I believe," he confirmed.

We'd done it. In a handful of hours we'd done what days of searching every bit of external MOME security footage couldn't do.

The bad news was, it was a mass of drab concrete with a giant parking lot beside it nestled in downtown Phoenix, a city that held over four million people. Meaning that if things went sideways, the very least that would happen was four million people going up in smoke (assuming we somehow avoided the whole "tearing a hole in time and space and imploding the universe" piece).

Luckily for me, our plan didn't leave me time to think about how terrifyingly wrong things could go.

Gwen added a few finishing touches to everyone's disguises—which she accomplished with a single wave of the hand that could just as easily have been a gesture of farewell, especially since she disappeared as soon as she finished the gesture—and then I was being dragged along just above the elbow, courtesy of a very stern-faced almost-Sol. Whatever Gwen had done made her look like a stranger, though she was a stranger who shared the same basic skin tone, hair type, and facial structure as Sol. She pulled Az along on her other side. We both did our best to move mechanically, imitating the way that Sol had described the motions of someone under a MOME arrest spell. Torrence, meanwhile, seemed to be doing his best to injure Seamus and Trevor as he dragged them by their collars into the building through the double set of glass doors that was so common for desert office entrances.

Watching him play the role of a violent enforcer who considered his four captives to be just so much shit under his boot was an education in acting. Either that, or he was totally going to kill us.

Torrence had slipped into the skin of a pissed off, unthinking muscle cop so well it was hard to believe he was actually the Unterberg council's lead intelligence officer. Trusting him made me more than a little nervous, but he'd had plenty of chances to kill us or let us die today, so I just had to hope he was actually on our side.

You'd think that after our last few MOME rescue initiatives, having Torrence and Sol pose as MOME officers wouldn't really be an option, but Sol had confirmed that more than one tauren already worked for the North American branch (bonus: she confirmed that tauren was the right word for what Torrence was) so he wouldn't look out of place despite being a large bull-person who looked like he could have just stepped out of a Greek myth. In addition, Trev had confirmed a few days prior that no major security protocols had changed in MOME's online database. Which meant that, while our Bolivian rescue ops might have caused a few word of mouth warnings for folks to keep an eye out for anyone strange, nothing had changed so much that two officers who looked familiar (thanks to Gwen's hastily applied illusions) bringing in a handful of nondescript law-breakers was going to attract undue attention, as long as we didn't stick around too long.

Not sticking around too long was going to be key.

And, yeah, ok, maybe Torrence was actually doing too good of a job of playing the asshole cop, or maybe Seamus was playing up the battered prisoner thing too much, because we'd only made it past the second security checkpoint—courtesy of some fake IDs Trev had cooked up for Sol and Torrence, and which Gwen had further modified—when an actual MOME security officer approached us. She was dressed in a grey pantsuit which, combined with her light skin and brown hair, made her completely unremarkable. I assumed she was a mage.

The expression on her face made it seem like one of us had stepped in dog crap on the way in, and only reinforced my guess that she was a mage. My brief experiences with MOME had taught me that mages in this line of work didn't think much of their shifter counterparts. Then again, maybe she just took issue with the man-bull who was dragging Seamus by the collar. Sol was holding my elbow instead, along with Az's. I tried to look at Az, but they had done something to themself to prevent anyone from more than glancing at them (it was the best way to keep them hidden in a place like this, because covering up the fact that they were a succubus was nigh impossible, no matter what kind of illusion one used), so I couldn't get a good look at their expression. Still, I didn't think they were too happy with the new scrutiny we were under either.

"Bullard, I'm going to need to talk to you for a minute," she said, addressing Torrence. I couldn't read his fake ID from here, but I doubt the mage could either. Apparently, Gwen had done a good enough job that this woman had mistaken him for some other tauren jerk, though.

"What, now?" Torrence asked, exuding the kind of disdain that spoke of either a personal history or a deep dislike of women in power. Torrence held firm to Seamus, shaking him angrily even as he spoke. But, at the same time, he pushed Trev towards me in a way that forced him to lightly jostle the grey suited mage. The glower she directed at Torrence intensified, but she didn't give Trev a second glance as Sol let go of Az's elbow to take Trev's instead.

Given my previous interactions with Torrence, his acrid tone was a bit of a shock, but apparently it was exactly the reaction that the grey-suited officer was expecting.

She nodded to Sol, dismissing her quickly, before rounding on Torrence.

Sol didn't hesitate. She turned on her heel and continued on down the hall with her three prisoners as if everything were perfectly normal.

"This is the third time this week that I've had to talk to you about the way you treat the people you're bringing in, Bullard. How am I supposed to…"

The security officer's voice faded out of hearing as Sol kept us moving down the hall.

Even so, I was deeply glad when Trev pulled us down a side hall leading to a closed, windowless black door. Trev swiped a keycard down the access panel next to the door and I had to restrain a shocked exclamation as I recognized the grey-suited mage in the photo ID attached to it. Trev had mentioned that the fake IDs wouldn't get us to the cameras he needed, he'd just never told us exactly how he'd planned to get ahold of a real one, only that he'd "handle it."

Probably a good thing. If I'd known that his plan had relied on mugging a real MOME agent, I might have objected.

For now my objections were put on hold, as, the moment the door swung open, we were faced with a small, dark room, full of security video feed—and vampires.

FORTUNATELY, WE HAD Azrael with us. Before the two closest vampires could even react to our presence, Azrael swooped in and dealt with all seven of them. It was really quite something to see Az work. The succubus moved so fast that it barely registered as motion. From the looks of things, all Az needed to get the better of a vampire was to get one hand on their bare skin. When I'd asked them to explain to the group about their vampire fighting superpowers, they'd said that their succubus nature simply pulled all the vamp's stolen energy away, and then they collapsed like rag dolls. Apparently, vamps were so easily drained because the energy wasn't theirs to begin with.

"Are they dead?" I asked, even as Trev stepped over the limp vampires to get to whatever controls he needed to access. "'Cause they seem dead."

Az looked at me, hand on their chest as if hurt, and they must have dropped whatever spell they'd used to keep my gaze away, because I was able to look back at them.

"You asked me not to kill them," they said.

"Yeah, well. Not everyone does what I ask, you know."

"They are vampires, Vic. They technically were dead before we started. However, these ones will regain themselves in a few hours' time."

Trev had gotten to work as soon as the vamps were down, and he was already immersed in pulling apart a few control panels and messing with wires.

"We have to go," said Sol, pulling on my arm.

I hesitated. We were going to need to leave Trev here to run things while we made our way to the dungeon, so he could keep security off of our tails for as long as possible. I hated it.

Az touched my arm.

"I'll stay here with him," they said. "I am an excellent defense against more than just vampires."

I nodded. That hadn't been the original plan, but it sounded a hell of a lot better than leaving Trev here by himself. Especially now that I'd seen how heavily guarded MOME was leaving their security feeds. It no longer seemed likely that Trev wouldn't have someone else from MOME drop in on him while he was trying to tell us how to get to Siara and evade more security personnel.

So, we left Trev to set up whatever relay he needed for Rhelia to do her thing, along with Az to help keep MOME security off of his back.

Meanwhile, I continued on with Sol.

I still didn't like the fact that Trev was here, and that we were leaving him behind, but I'd be doing the same thing to him that he'd tried to do to Rhelia if I attempted to stop him. I still hated having him so close to MOME again after everything they'd done to him, all that they'd tried to do him, had wanted to do to him. It made me pretty ragey just thinking about it, but I pushed those thoughts aside and focused on looking like a frightened prisoner. It wasn't a big stretch, to be honest.

Even without the extra help from Torrence, getting into a MOME headquarters never seemed to be a problem for us. Getting out was usually the challenge, and this time I couldn't shake the feeling that we were going to be caught at any moment. If things went badly this time around the results would be catastrophic, not just for me and the people I loved, but for the entire Phoenix metro area, possibly the world, and if we were especially unlucky, maybe even the universe. So… no, acting wasn't really required to get my palms sweating and my stomach feeling like it was about to jump out of my mouth to parachute someplace safe.

Except if we failed today there might not be a safe place, like, anywhere, and I was really just going to have to stop thinking about failure, because it was doing me no damned good.

Sol was clearly dragging out our walk as we waited for Trev to patch Rhelia through so that she could confirm that the dungeons were indeed where Siara was being held, not to mention tell us how the hells to get there.

Seamus and I had been here exactly once before, and we'd been blindfolded and unconscious on the way in, and too nervous to see straight on the way out. We were about as helpful as a service dog with a sinus infection. Apparently, the only thing Sol could think of to draw things out was to shake me while talking smack periodically. This seemed so unlike her that it was almost humorous.

Except that her cuffs up the side of my head were getting difficult to ignore. I was just considering ways to retaliate the next time she hit me, when I heard Trev's voice in my head.

We're in, Vic. Rhelia has the location. Head southwest to the next major intersection of corridors, then turn right.

Roger that.

"Are you taking me to the dungeons or what?" I said aloud, as Sol readied another blow. "You're a lot of talk for someone who isn't even taking me to interrogation."

"Shut up," Sol grumbled.

Basement, sub-section six, Trev relayed mentally.

I tripped then, and Sol had to bend down to catch me, so that her face was right next to mine.

"Basement, sub-section six," I whispered, while she was there.

Hopefully, with no one right next to us, and Trev dutifully pointing the security cameras elsewhere, no one would notice.

I let Sol drag me down the hall, while my brain wandered for a moment to how strange it was that Gwen always showed up just in time to cast a major illusion spell for us before any major mission. I mean, seriously, she almost never missed the chance. This was the first time I'd thought of it, and I would bet money that if I tried to PLAN on Gwen showing up at the last minute to cast such a spell it would never work out, but still, it was weird how consistent she was.

I am the Goddess of fortune, my dear.

Odd. That had sounded like Gwen's voice, but I'd never had Gwen's voice in my head before.

I hear you whenever you think of me, Vic, but I rarely answer. You seem unusually troubled, though, so I thought I would check in.

Strange that she thought I was more troubled than usual. I mean, I was just thinking about her consistently random timing for saving our butts, she was a literal deus ex machina, and that was kind of funny when you thought about it.

You are so desperately trying not to think about what you are about to do, that I can sense your distress even from here.

Well, I think I'm doing a pretty good job coping, all things considered, I thought reproachfully.

Yes. You are admirably placing one foot in front of the other and marching directly into the lion's den. It is to be respected. I should warn you, though, I'm rather busy at the moment. There are many threads being pulled right now. I can't promise to be there if you need me. I strongly recommend solving this one yourself, if at all possible.

There was something more important than Rebecca Dryer possibly destroying the entire universe by injecting an incredibly powerful weredragon with technetium right now? Hot damn. The shit must really be about to hit the fan on a global level.

You have no idea, dear. There's a reason that I have one of my best agents assigned to this mission in my place.

Oh? Who did you send?

I could feel relief wash over me as the meaning of Gwen's words sank in. Someone with Gwen's powers would be here. Someone Gwen trusted. Gwen didn't always get the little things right, like personal space, or freedom of choice, but she had yet to screw up any of the big things, like letting us die. I sensed some of the tension in my shoulders release for a moment, until Gwen's voice in my mind said, You, Vic. I sent you.

Me? What? How am I possibly your best agent? I just started. I have no idea what I'm doing, I—

Have managed to keep everyone you love from dying on multiple occasions. I have complete faith in you. Must go, there's a Russian leader that is in desperate need of being knocked off his horse.

Gwen?

Hello?

Did you seriously just ditch me to knock Putin on his ass?

Gwen didn't reply, and I wondered if she was just deflecting my curiosity with a weird story, or if it was actually somehow important to maintaining the fabric of the universe that she knock Russian dictators on their butts. Honestly, with Gwen it was impossible to know. One thing was clear—I was on my own.

I took a deep breath as Sol shoved me into an elevator, mashed in a security code I recited to her via Trev's voice in my mind, and then hit the button for the bottom.

Gwen believed in me. That had to count for something. Besides, our plan wasn't completely crazy. The things that could go wrong were fairly unlikely at this point, and even if things went wrong, the chances that events would lead to Siara getting injected with technetium here inside the MOME facility were pretty low. The people guarding her would have to be incredibly stupid for that to happen.

"NO, NO, NO. Put. That. Down. You won't just kill her, you'll kill all of us, along with everyone in this whole city, and possibly the entire earth. Seriously. Stop freaking out. Just put the needle down." I was doing my best not to shout, but I was going to fail any second now.

"You're lying! MOME wouldn't risk that! Why would they give us these suits if that were true? This suit wouldn't protect us against what you're describing. They wouldn't protect us at all."

I decided that shouting, "No shit, Sherlock! They don't care about you, and killing you is just part of their fucking evil scheme," wasn't going to help defuse the situation. Instead, I opted for putting my hands at my sides, palms out, and trying to use my calmest voice possible. I tried to look the shaky young man in the eyes, even through the thin rubber hazmat suit that enveloped him, but it was hard to see him behind the flickering light that reflected off the clear part covering his face.

"It's possible that MOME have decided to sacrifice a few for the sake of the many," I hedged, hoping that the dude an inch away from killing us all wasn't completely devoid of reason. "But let's say I'm wrong. Let's say all it's going to do is kill the woman you have your arm around. Does she really deserve to die right now? Is that really your call? Do you really think your bosses want her injected right here without any witnesses? Didn't they order for her to be taken up for a public execution?"

Dude just blinked at me for a full ten seconds before shuffling backwards again, as we both heard the shouts and scuffling of Sol fighting the other guards farther up the passage. With Trev and Rhelia's help, we'd managed to avoid every single MOME employee on the way down here. Then, not long after we'd descended past eggshell painted walls, linoleum floors, and cheap fluorescent lights into coarse stone everything and torch sconces, we'd basically smacked face first into Siara's entourage, which had appeared to be in the process of taking her to the surface in order to inject her somewhere more public than the dungeon below a secret facility. We must have come upon them right after they'd grabbed her, because I could see the metal bars that marked the very same dungeon I'd been kept in during my "stay" here, just behind the guy who had a needle three centimeters from Siara's neck.

Trev had warned us that they were coming up, but not with enough time to hide before they reached us. Regardless, we didn't want them making it out of here. It seemed unlikely that their reinforcements would come from inside the dungeon, and as long as we were still inside these stone walls, no one could use their dark matter. Sol and I had both been trained to fight without magic, but past experience suggested most MOME officers weren't.

So, pressing what little advantage we had, Sol had engaged the guards at the front of the line and I had sprinted to the back to try to get Siara away from the two MOME agents in hazmat suits who were dragging her shackled form through the dark stone halls. If I hadn't known for a fact that Rhelia wasn't in Phoenix I would have had a brief panic attack thinking that she had somehow been captured. I almost did anyway, until I remembered that Siara was a dead ringer for her granddaughter, down to the iridescence of her ebon skin. The only difference between them that I could see was that Siara's eyes were green instead of yellow. I tried to calm my breathing even as I ran down the tunnel. There were no other prisoners in sight, so I had to assume that Emil wasn't a part of today's entertainment.

I had a fair bit of momentum going when I skidded to a stop in front of Siara's guards, so I'd used that to turn and kick the first guard in the head hard enough that he bounced off the wall and slumped to the ground before he'd even really known what was going on. The second guy had pulled Siara in front of him like a hostage and put the needle uncomfortably close to her neck.

Now, as I watched this panicky minion who apparently had never bothered to question his evil overlords before, the needle's point dipped dangerously close to Siara's skin. I wondered if he'd been the one assigned to inject her with technetium once they reached the surface, or if they'd all been equipped with syringes just in case things went south. The latter thought was truly terrifying, but I couldn't imagine how else this trembling cowpie of a human being could possibly have reached the conclusion that he ought to inject technetium into a weredragon inside of his own employer's U.S. headquarters.

My palms were already sweating from resisting the urge to launch myself at this rubber-wrapped asshat, but I dug my nails into my palms as I did my best not to raise my arms and shout threatening things at him as well. One false sway of the wrist and that needle would be in her neck. From there, all it would take would be—

Oh. Fuck.

In the blink of an eye, all my worst nightmares were realized. That needle entering the skin of one of the most powerful weredragons in the world was going to erase everything. Everything. Everyone I loved most in the world was right here in this building, and injecting Siara with a dose of technetium would likely destroy the entirety of the Phoenix metro area. Almost five million people gone in the blink of an eye, along with maybe the entire earth, but especially my brother and my two best friends. I didn't have time to process what I was doing. Didn't really have time to think anything, but the options were pretty simple: Option 1: Do nothing and let everyone I care about, including myself, die horribly, along with many people I didn't even know. Option 2: Launch myself at the asshat holding the needle and the woman he was trying to kill, reach for whatever magic I could, and hope it made things better. I didn't really see how it could make anything worse.

I heard multiple people yelling as I leapt the short distance between me and my target, but I couldn't really process anything that was being said. My eyes were focused on Siara's pupils, which told me all that I needed to know, and I saw them dilate with the shock of the needle puncturing her skin, and perhaps the feeling of technetium entering her veins. I barely noticed as hazmat moron pushed himself away from her, as if that would somehow save him. As if the flimsy rubber that covered him could serve as any kind of protection from what he'd just done. I certainly didn't process any of the shouts from around me. I did my best to ignore Trev's mental cry of my name, as I threw myself on top of Siara and reached with everything in me for what I hoped would be there.

Just barely there. Just the edge of time. A fold in the fabric of space. I pulled.

Blackness took over.

WHEN I OPENED my eyes, lying on my back in the sands of a narrow red canyon, looking up at a small stretch of orange sky, I almost cried with relief. Instead, my body did one weirder and I started laughing hysterically. I guess thinking you were about to die, along with everyone you love, and then not, can do that to you.

"How are we alive?" Siara asked.

I almost countered that I wasn't entirely sure that we were, but then I rose up to my elbows and took in just how rough she looked—raven hair a curled, matted mess, skin a shade of charcoal rather than the deep ebony it normally was, reptilian irises still dilated and sclera red from… well, from the shit we were still going through, I supposed.

"How do you feel?" I asked. When Siara simply stared at me, I realized that maybe she really needed an answer to her question before she could answer mine. "I'm not 100% positive, but my understanding is that there is something about this canyon that completely suppresses dark matter. Not just mostly, like the dungeon at MOME, but completely."

"But why would that stop the Technetium from blowing me up?"

"Well, keep in mind I didn't really plan this, I just dove at you and hoped like hell my subconscious brain knew what it was doing. But now that we're here and I can think about it, my best guess is that the Technetium can't react with the dark matter because it's being so suppressed it might as well not be in your blood stream."

"So… I'm trapped here?"

I shrugged.

"Maybe. Sure beats dying and taking the whole world down with you though, doesn't it?" I said, collapsing to the floor of the canyon again as I realized just how fucking lucky I'd been.

I giggled again.

"You find this funny?" Siara asked, allowing her own legs to give out and joining me on the sandy canyon floor.

I shook my head as the giggles turned into raucous laughter once more.

"Nope," I said when I could manage enough air. "I just think my body and brain are freaking out about how close we came to dying just now."

Siara lay down and looked at the sky.

"Why is the sky orange?" she asked.

"No idea. That wasn't part of my orientation. And before you ask, no, I have no clue why it smells like sulphur here either. Or why the sun is purple, not that you can see the sun right now. Also, we probably need to get on our feet as soon as possible because the floods here happen every few hours and we need to find somewhere for you to not drown while you're here."

I got up and started brushing the sand off of my legs.

Siara remained lying down.

"Now isn't a great time for a nap, Siara," I said.

"Perhaps I should simply remain here and let the waters take me," she replied.

I sighed.

"Right. I guess living in this canyon for the re-mainder of what is likely to be a few more centuries of life probably doesn't appeal much. I get that."

"Do you, child? Do you understand the eternity that faces most of dragon-kind? Rhelia and my family are not just weredragons, we have ancestors who are pure dragons as well. That is why we look as we do, and not as you do. We are likely to live for millennia, if nothing brings us down before then."

I forced my mouth closed and tried to breathe through my nose.

"Ok. Did not know that, but it explains a lot, thanks. However, it doesn't change what I was about to say."

"Which was?"

"Which was that if you let the flash floods carry you to the bottom of the canyon, I have it on good authority that MOME has a net or something that catches people and zaps them back to the facility we just left."

"Which means that I would be returned to a place where my dark matter would once more engage with the Technetium in my blood?"

"Yep. And then you're right back to killing everyone in Phoenix and possibly the world."

Siara sighed and then stood up and punched the canyon wall. The resounding crack, and the shudder that reverberated the canyon, was even more startling than the revelation of the lifespan of dragon kind. I looked up to see if we were about to be killed by rock fall, but luckily, aside from the cracks that radiated away from the impact point of Siara's fist, everything looked stable.

"What are the chances that being dead would prevent the Technetium from having its desired effect?" she asked.

I wondered when I had suddenly become an expert on Technetium and its reactions with dark matter, or why Siara thought I knew more about it than she did, but then I remembered Trev talking about how some of the oldest magical beings had the hardest time coming to terms with the science behind dark matter manipulation. For them, the powers they wielded had always been innate and natural. You could do what you could do, and you couldn't do what you couldn't do, and you didn't question the gifts you'd been given or lacked. You simply lived your life breathing magic and sweating spells, and didn't question how any of it all fit together. According to him, anyway. I wasn't sure that Siara was particularly tied to tradition, or even averse to knowing how dark matter worked. Still, it made sense that after however many centuries, or millennia she might have already lived with magic just working without having to worry about the how and why, she might want help sorting out how these new ideas worked, and more importantly, what they meant right now.

"I mean, again, I'm just guessing here, but I would think that the moment your blood, laced with Technetium, returned to a place where the dark matter was no longer suppressed, the two would mix and react, annihilating… everything within a very large radius, possibly taking the whole universe down with it, especially considering how close this seam would be when you exploded."

"You don't have to preface everything you say with the fact that you are just guessing. I have internalized the fact that you are not an expert in this particular subject, but you are the closest that I have to an expert at the moment."

I nodded and sighed. That was still a lot of pressure, but at least Siara acknowledged that I was mostly talking out of my ass.

"Look, I don't know what the long term solution is, but there must be something other than, 'Live here in this canyon for the rest of your very long existence.' We just have to figure out what that is. In the meantime, we need to find you a place that won't let you get swept away with the next flood."

"Where did you go when you escaped?"

"I climbed to the top of the canyon after removing my manacles and shit," which made me do a double take when I looked at Siara. "Where are your manacles, by the way?" I asked.

She looked at her wrists and ankles and then tilted her head to one side.

"No idea. They have not been here since we arrived. Though they were certainly keeping me from destroying that dimwitted MOME agent in the dungeons."

"Weird."

"How did you arrive here the first time?" Siara asked.

"A MOME agent brought me here and left me in the canyon," I said, thinking back. "Come to think of it, that lady brought me here and put a new set of manacles on me as soon as we arrived, saying they would keep me from using my magic."

"And did they?"

I considered for a moment.

"Well, I thought they did, because my magic wouldn't work, but after I got to the top Azrael said that was the canyon and not the manacles."

"So she probably brought them simply to make certain that you were restrained," Siara surmised. "Certain seams will not allow people through if they are restrained, others remove the restraints."

"Really? How does that work?"

"I do not know, youngling. I only know that it is true."

"That makes seams sound sentient," I said, feeling decidedly creeped out by the idea.

Siara shrugged.

"Many things in the universe have a form of consciousness. Perhaps seams do as well."

And with that, Siara stood up and started walking away from me.

"Siara," I said, causing her to turn and look back at me over her shoulder. I was about to tell her that she was headed the wrong way, that she had started walking in the direction of the "trap" that MOME had set for anyone caught in the floods, but those words died on my tongue.

"What in the hells is that?" I asked instead, as something blotted out what little portion of the orange sky could be seen from the bottom of the narrow canyon in which we stood, and a horrible screeching filled the air.

17

"YOU BRILLIANT, BRILLIANT, genius of a woman!"

That was what I chose to believe Azrael was screeching at me as their red-skinned, fluff-tailed body came flying at my head from the sky. But of course, since we were once more in the canyon, and Azrael was in their demon form, I could only hear what sounded like a banshee and a demented cat having a screaming match.

"What is that?" Siara asked, her nose wrinkling as though Azrael had brought more of the sulfurous stench with them, while the creature collided with my torso and knocked me back into the canyon sand.

"It's Azrael," I said, once I could breathe again. Siara only a raised a single eyebrow at me. "The succubus who was helping us back on Earth?" I clarified. "They helped us find you. They were keeping the vampires busy while we came to your rescue."

That didn't seem to do much for Siara in terms of a memory jog, so I just shrugged and returned the manic embrace that the squirrel demon had me in.

"I think I saw that whole shadow thing you were talking about, Az," I said, not knowing what else to talk about. "You blotted out the sun completely, and it wasn't just lucky positioning. You were HUGE."

Azrael nestled up against my ear and then pulled emphatically on my ear lobe. I didn't know what that meant, but decided it was supposed to be affectionate and patted their head in response.

"Where is everyone else?" I asked, after a brief pause for squirrely affection. And then I wanted to smack my head against the wall of the canyon because the response was, of course, a heinous shrieking directly into my ear.

"Never mind!" I shouted. "You can tell me later. Maybe we can play charades for now? Please remember that I can't understand you down here."

Azrael nodded once and shrugged. Then they leapt from my shoulder and ran off down the canyon.

"Az, wait!" I shouted, but their four legged form was hustling away from me with a hustle that seemed less than casual. "We'd better follow them."

"Don't you mean, him?" she asked, gesturing at Az's retreating form. And yeah, Az looked decidedly male in their naked squirrel demon form, but…

"I should ask if they want me to change pronouns when they're in demon squirrel form. Az has never expressed a preference, actually. They never correct anyone who chooses he or she, but they seemed pleased when I started using 'them.' Still, I should really ask."

It wasn't as if I'd had a ton of time to kick back with Az and talk preferred pronouns, but even so, it was only polite. I needed to make time.

Siara looked at me briefly, then shrugged and hustled after the red-skinned squirrel demon. She moved quickly and with purpose, but there was something about her gait that seemed off. I wondered if she was injured from her time in the dungeons, or if perhaps the reaction between the Technetium and dark matter was only slowed down by the canyon, and not completely stopped. That was a terrifying thought. Deciding there was nothing I could do about it either way, I hurried after Siara and the quickly fading shape of Azrael the squirrel demon.

~~~

"This isn't working, Az."

I shook my head again, as I failed, for the hundredth time, to turn Az's jerky, random motions into some sort of coherent meaning.

"A cat is being mangled repeatedly in a washing machine?" Siara guessed for the third time.

"If that wasn't right the last two times, why would it suddenly be right this time?" I asked.

She shrugged.

"That's just what it looks like."

She wasn't wrong.

"Az, seriously. We have no idea what you're trying to say. How can you be this bad at charades?"

Az leveled their gaze at me and gestured their tiny squirrel hands up and down their red-skinned squirrel body.

"Ok. Fair point, well made. You aren't exactly built for the human game in this body," I admitted.
~~~

Azrael collapsed in a heap on the tiny rock ledge that formed the "balcony" of the small cave (cave was a generous term, it was more of a slight indentation in the cliff side) that would be Siara's shelter for the foreseeable future. Since Az had led us up here and then proceeded to shoo us inside the small depression, I didn't think they were trying to warn us of some terrible fate. But I couldn't for the life of me figure out what they were trying to tell us.

"If I am going to marooned here with that creature, I am likely to fling one of us from this cliff ledge."

That garnered cold looks from both Az and me.

"That squirrel is more difficult to communicate with than General Aira, and she is a dragon who speaks in three word sentences and acts as though emotions are things that only plague other people."

"I'm starting to get the impression you're not a huge fan of your general," I offered, happy to talk about something other than the ways in which she was annoyed by Az.

Siara sighed.

"She is very good at her job. However, she is blinded by her prejudices and her own past."

I chuckled a bit.

"She sounds pretty human," I offered.

Siara's mouth curved up, on one side only.

"Do not tell her you think so," she advised. "She is entirely dragon, though she has a human form she takes often enough when it suits her."

I wasn't sure I'd ever heard of full dragons taking human form before, but given what I'd just learned about Siara's ancestry, it made sense. Dragons mating with humans in dragon form sounded… awkward. I shook my head, and decided to add it to the pile of things I would ask about later. Right now I needed to do my best to keep Siara safe and alive.

I took a deep breath, looking between the exasperated squirrel demon and the overwhelmed weredragon. I had a feeling I was going to regret this later, but…

"Siara, are you ok if I leave you here for a bit?" I asked.

Siara looked pointedly down at the bottom of the canyon and then up towards the top.

"Where exactly do you think you're going?"

I sighed.

"Unfortunately, I think the only way we can figure out what Az is trying to say is if I climb out of here and let the translation magic that normally works in this realm kick in. Then I'll have to climb back down here and tell you whatever it is."

At my words Az sat up and began nodding enthusiastically.

"This had better be as important as you're making it seem," I muttered to them.

Siara looked at me as though I'd started growing a second head.

"What?" I asked, not entirely sure I hadn't started growing another head. My life had been so batshit nuts lately, and this realm was so much weirder than most, that I would hardly have been surprised.

"It seems a great risk to take," she said, and I could tell she was leaving something unsaid.

"If you think I shouldn't take the trouble to go up there and come back down, because you're planning to just die down here and save everyone the trouble, then we are going to have to have words when I come back," I said, channeling my own mother as best I could, an effort I had never made before, but suddenly found all too fitting. "You're Rhelia's family, and mine, now. If you think I'm just going to leave you here to rot, you've got another think coming."

Siara turned away and stared at the back wall of the cave for a moment.

"Victoria, I would not forgive myself if something were to happen to you while you were trying to assist me."

I shrugged and stood up.

"And I won't forgive myself if I don't find out what Az is trying to say and it winds up being information that could save your life. So, we're at an impasse and, as only one of us can leave this place without taking the whole universe down with her, I guess you'll just have to hang out here while I try not to die. Ok?'

Siara smirked and nodded.

"You are more like your mother than I first supposed," she said.

Which felt like a punch directly in the gut.

"You knew my Mom?" I asked, sitting down again without really meaning to.

Siara raised an eyebrow.

"You didn't know that?" she asked.

I put my head in my hands.

"My parents never told me anything about this world, about magic or shifting, or any of it before they… disappeared." I was going to say died, but I found the word harder and harder to form these days, as everything about their death—and lives, for that matter—seemed less and less clear.

"I knew that, but… surely Rhelia or Trevor mentioned—" she looked at me and started shaking her head back and forth, as though trying to shrug off some insect that buzzed her head. "Those children… honestly… they are far too used to keeping secrets for my liking. I understand the necessity at times, but this? Why wouldn't they tell you?"

No longer having any clue what we were talking about, I just stared at her, wide-eyed, reminding myself to blink.

"Your parents sought refuge in the dragon realm for a time, in their attempts to evade MOME, before they… disappeared."

I noticed that she used the same word I had, but more cautiously, as though she wasn't sure what its exact meaning was.

"How long before they disappeared?" I asked, wondering how much more of my parents' lives I knew nothing about.

"Months. The dragon realm is barred to anyone who isn't led there by someone who is dragonkin. My ancestors chose it for that purpose eons ago, or so the stories say. It makes an excellent hiding place for those trying to avoid an association like MOME—one that is decidedly unpopular with all dragon kind. Unfortunately, your parents eventually decided that their presence in our realm was too great a risk. I am not clear on their exact thinking, but I got the impression they were worried that MOME would figure out a way into our realm and hurt us in an attempt to get their hands on your parents. I never understood how they thought such a thing was possible, but I believe it is what led them to abandon the dragon realm and continue their circumnavigation."

I really wanted to ask a hundred other questions, but Az was jumping up and down like a kangaroo on a pogo stick and gesturing wildly at the top of the cliff.

"We need to continue this conversation," I said, looking between Az and the top of the canyon, or at least the line between the rock and the sky. "But apparently I need to get my ass in gear."

Az nodded emphatically, and Siara merely sighed and nodded towards the cliff face.

"Good luck, Victoria."

"I'll be back soon."

If only I'd known how big a lie that was.

THE CLIMB TO the top of the canyon was substantially less exciting this time than it had been the last time. For one thing, the red-skinned squirrel demon did not launch itself at my head this time. For another, I wasn't completely haggard from days without food or water, exposure to the elements, and breaking out of my bonds. Instead, I was just a bit tired from our master escape plan of the night. My whole body felt somewhat heavy with exertion and my scars pulled periodically as I stretched for some of the farther holds on the way up but, for the most part, the climbing was smooth and steady. Also, perhaps most importantly, I knew what awaited me at the top, so I wasn't constantly checking the horizon to make sure nothing was trying to kill me from above.

In retrospect, that might have been a mistake.

Regardless, I made much better time than my previous ascent, and reached the top only partially exhausted, though not at all looking forward to the downclimb that would return me to Siara's ledge.

"Ok, Az," I huffed out, as I collapsed a few feet from the edge of the cliff it had taken me two hours to ascend. "What the fuck is going on?"

"First of all, can I just say how bloody brilliant you are for thinking of this canyon? I don't know if I would have come up with that on such short notice, and I live here."

"Thank my subconscious. That was a blind leap for me, I reached for the seam and hoped for the best. I guess some part of my brain remembered that the canyon suppresses dark matter, but honestly, that wasn't a conscious thought of mine when I grabbed Siara. I was just desperate to keep everyone I loved from dying."

Azrael poked his long, red nose in my face from above where I lay.

"Are you telling me that you grabbed her, expecting to die, and just did your best to take her somewhere else so that she might not kill the rest of us?"

I grimaced and nodded. It had been one of the dumbest things I'd ever done, but I hadn't seen any choice really, and then I'd been incredibly lucky. Or maybe part of me had suspected what would happen. Who knows.

"You absolutely moronic, lovely, brave, mad individual!" Azrael was bouncing up and down on my chest now, too light to knock the wind from my lungs, but not particularly comfortable either. They were rather large for a squirrel. I sat up when they latched onto my shoulder in a way that I assumed was supposed to be a hug, but it was difficult to tell, and one small squirrel hand was far too close to my boob for my liking.

"Thanks? I guess. Look, I'll admit it might have been mad, and was probably stupid, but what else was I supposed to do?"

"Nothing! Die horribly, I suppose? I dunno. But I'm very glad that you did what you did."

"Look, Az, I appreciate the love fest and all, but what were you trying to tell us earlier? It seemed important."

Az blinked for a moment.

"Oh yes, that. Mostly I just wanted to get you up here to talk to you, but I was trying to say that the spot Siara is in could be good for the long term, as the next time there's a stampede it will likely provide her with some much needed food. Quite a few of the folks who run from the storms fall into that canyon."

I stared at them for a moment and blinked.

"You made me climb to the top of this canyon to mention that there might be falling snacks?"

"Well, yes. It will be enough to keep her alive and keep her from attempting to leave the canyon before it's safe for her."

"But... I climbed for two hours, Az. TWO HOURS! So you could tell us about snacks? What if I'd fallen? What if I'd fallen and wiped out Siara on my way down? Seriously? How could you be so bad at charades that you couldn't manage to sign FOOD?!" I held up a hand and made the Earth-wide accepted gesture for food—sandwiched fingers towards a mouth making eating motions. Then I sighed, thinking about how far I'd climbed and how much farther I'd have to downclimb just to deliver the message: beware of falling snacks. "I can't believe you brought me up here just for that."

Az's squirrel form frowned, and it booped its elongated red nose against mine.

"I brought you up here so I could tell you that you'd better start workin' out how to get yourself home, 'cause everyone thinks you're dead, Luv."

I just stared at Az for a moment.

"You didn't tell them where you were going when you left?" I asked.

Az shrugged.

"I came here on a guess, Luv. After the world didn't explode, and we made our way back out of that damned concrete dungeon."

"Thought I left you on the upper floors?"

"The whole bloody building's a dungeon, love. No better word for that many cubicles."

Az's whole squirrel body shuddered and I was forced to laugh.

"I did join the fray in the basement, though," Az added, after a moment.

"Oh?"

"Well, Trev was screaming his bloody head off as soon as you disappeared, and then it was only a matter of time before the jig was up, so we ran to meet Sol, and the bull and wolf joined us on the way down. Everyone was cryin' and fightin' and determined to find Emil before they left, but... I ran to the seam and decided to test a theory."

"So, they really think I'm dead?"

Az nodded, somberly.

"I had a hunch, though. Thought that you might have headed here and that you might need my help. Didn't want to get anyone's hopes up, though, so I just told them I'd be back when I could."

I was quiet for a bit as I considered all the implications of that. I didn't like the idea of my friends thinking I was dead. I knew firsthand how painful it was to lose someone close to you. I didn't want them feeling that kind of grief, if they didn't have to. But for now I had other things to worry about.

"Az, what am I going to do for her? Just because she won't starve thanks to your falling snacks, that doesn't mean she'll survive... or want to. How can we fix this?"

Azrael's long nose twitched a few times before they spoke again.

"I honestly don't know, Luv. This is all new to me. I'd never heard of Technetium until you explained things to me after that first time MOME blew a bunch of folks up. I don't know how to reverse that kind of thing, but at least she won't die right away and take the whole world down with her, eh? Nice if we can put off the end of the universe for a little while longer, innit?"

"Why do you sound more human in your squirrel form?" I asked, unable to miss how Azrael's accent had thickened the more we'd sat talking at the top of this cliff.

"Dunno, could just be your perception of me. After all, you're not even listenin' to me speak really, just a translation of what I'm saying in demon. Maybe I jus' seem more human to you now?"

"But you aren't actually from South London, so the accent is put on anyway, at least it is when you have vocal chords, so why on Earth would I—oh fuck it, who cares? Is that all you had for me? I suppose I should be getting back to inform Siara about her meal plan."

Az began to nod, then turned, eyes growing wide with horror, as an ominous thundering rolled in from the distance.

"Az? What is that?"

"That, Luv, is our cue to leave."

I shuffled myself towards the cliff ledge, getting ready to climb down to Siara's cave again.

"Not that way, Luv. We need to get through the nearest seam and get out of here."

"I can't leave Siara down there," I said, turning towards Az for a moment, mentally preparing myself for the climb down, all the while.

"Vic, stop! Don't be ridiculous! You can't get to her before the stampede gets here, and you'll never make that climb without taking a falling demon to the head. You'll just get killed and have nothing to show for it."

"I can't just leave her here, Az!" I said, lying down and dangling my feet over the edge to start my descent.

"You can come back!" Az shouted. He had to shout now to be heard over the distant rumbling. A rumbling that was getting terrifyingly less distant with each second. "You can take the seam out of here and come back in an hour and they'll be gone! But if you stay here, you'll die. Siara has that cave for cover, the demons won't kill her unless she's too dim to duck in when she hears the stampede. She doesn't seem dim to me. Please Vic, believe me, you do not want to be stuck on that cliff when they get here."

Az's face was so earnest, such a tiny, squirrelish vision of concern, that I had to take his words seriously for a moment. Then something occurred to me.

"Are you just saving your own ass, Az? Because I know you can't get out of here without help."

Their eyes widened, but before they could protest, the wave of sound that had been slowly approaching crested a hill behind us and I saw a black sea of... writhing life? Demons? I couldn't tell what it was exactly, but it was moving towards us far faster than I would have believed possible. I couldn't make out individual shapes in the mass, but it was quite clear that nothing in the path of that wall of living creatures would be spared.

Before I could think about it again, I pulled myself up from the ledge, snatched Az from the ground in front of me, and reached for the nearest fold in spacetime.

I'm sorry, Siara. I'll try to be back soon. Watch out for falling snacks.

I HAD EXPECTED to find myself back in the same MOME dungeon I'd snatched Siara from. After all, the last time I'd used the seam at the top of the canyon in Az's realm, that's where I'd wound up. Instead, I found myself standing in a giant green field, waist deep in waving rows of a grain I wasn't familiar with, but which could easily have been wheat.

The sky was blue again, so we definitely weren't in Azrael's realm, but beyond that I had no idea where we were. The air smelled of earth and plants. The sun was warm on my skin, and the only thing I could see, as far as the horizon, was grain.

"Well… this is new…" I muttered, as I turned to look from the landscape to Azrael, who had been in my arms as we'd arrived. They were no longer in my arms. They were also no longer Azrael. Or rather, instead of a red furless squirrel or a winged humanoid, I now stood a few feet away from an enormous death omen.

Since no one else was around, I was pretty sure it was Azrael.

"That's different," I said, taking in all of maybe-Azrael's latest body.

Maybe-Azrael seemed to be a raven, except they were a raven that was at least a head taller than I was, and proportioned accordingly.

Caw.

"Let me guess," I said, still staring at the feathers that were so deep a black they had a blue sheen to them. "There's no translation magic in this realm."

Caw caw.

"Well, at least you don't sound like a dying cat every time you open your mouth," I replied with a sigh. The giant raven's feathers ruffled, and it snapped its beak angrily, making me fairly certain it was indeed Azrael who stood before me.

"One of these days, you'll have to explain to me why your form manifests so differently in every realm," I said, as I turned my head to the sky to take in our surroundings more clearly. It was going to be damned annoying that Azrael couldn't explain things to me here. Which made me even more certain that Azrael was now a giant raven, because of course they would be. This is my life we're talking about, and if it ain't inconvenient and weird, it's trying to kill me.

I had no idea where we were, but as long as nothing terrible happened, I supposed we just needed to wait an hour and then I could just find the seam that had brought us here and take it back.

"I suppose I should just make sure I know where that seam is," I muttered, mostly to myself, as I stretched my hands out in front of me and felt for the fold in space and time that would get us out of here. "Just to be certain we can get back easily once we've waited out the stampede."

CAW CAW CAW CAW CAW!

I turned to look at Azrael, even as I felt my fingers hum with the energy of the seam that had brought us here.

"What?" I asked, concerned by the frantic tone to Azrael's cawing.

Caw.

Azrael's last caw had contained a finality that sent a shiver down my spine, and when I turned to look at them, their eyes were gazing skyward at a spot in the distance.

A spot that was getting larger.

"Az… what's that?" I asked, even though I knew the raven couldn't answer me, at least not in a way that I could understand.

Caw.

Az hopped to my side, collapsing a swath of wheat in their wake, and hunkered down in a gesture that made it all too clear that I should get on their back.

I scoffed at that, and reached for my dragon form instead. Az wasn't the only one with wings here. I closed my eyes and imagined the rush of air beneath my wings, the feeling of a mouth filled with fangs that could rend an entire cow in a single bite, a belly full of fire hot enough to melt a vampire's skull, and…

Nothing. Nothing happened. Nothing changed.

Caw, caw, CAW.

Az was sounding more than a little bit anxious. I looked up and saw that the distant spot was now much larger, and I decided that having my own wings wasn't worth getting caught by whatever was coming for us. I climbed onto Azrael's back and clung on for dear life as the giant raven's wings flapped in an ever more hurried attempt to get us airborne.

After a few heartbeats, Az shot us skyward. For a second I worried that I would slide right off their back, but then they evened out and we were aloft, streaking over the great field of grain and then over a forest that must have been just out of sight from the field we'd started in. Az put on a burst of speed I would never have though possible for a raven. Of course, I'd never seen a raven this large before, so it could just have come down to the physics of a raven about fifty times bigger than average. Though, when I thought about it that way, I wondered if it should be physically possible for a raven that size to actually fly. I quickly abandoned that line of thinking, however, since Az was clearly flying whether physics liked it or not, and whatever had been coming for us was beginning to catch up.

As I looked over my shoulder I could see the shape of what had once been a burgeoning black dot on the horizon materialize into a cloud of wings and glinting metal behind us.

"That looks bad," I admitted, even as I hunkered closer to Az's shoulders. "Any chance you can go faster?" I asked, trying to keep the panic out of my voice. I didn't know if it would faze Az at all, but panicking generally didn't help anything and I knew it could be as contagious as a bad STI.

Caw.

It was a grumble that I wouldn't have been able to hear at all over the sound of the wind in my ears, but as I was pressed tight against Az's avian form, I felt it in my chest.

Panic or no, the vocalization made it clear I wasn't helping.

And soon enough I didn't have to worry about panic, or Az, or anything else except how I was about to die, because something large, winged, and screaming like a squirrel demon hopped up on cocaine dove from the sky and collided with me, knocking me off Az's back and sending me tumbling through the air.

ZRAEL DOVE FOR me. Since I was falling to my death back first, I could see them tuck their wings to their sides and plunge away from the attacking winged warriors that were encircling them as I fell, but I knew enough about physics to know that they wouldn't reach me in time. We hadn't been that far off the ground—only a couple thousand feet. Not the tens of thousands of feet needed for Az to have time to reach me before I hit the ground.

I tried to reach for my dragon form, my snow leopard form, some random magic that might keep me alive or help me save myself, but nothing responded. It didn't quite feel like being in the canyon in Az's realm, but I couldn't place how it was different, and didn't have the fucking time to worry about it, anyway. I was about to die, and I couldn't use my magic, that much was clear. Then, out of the corner of my eye, through the hair that had been ripped from its holder and was now flapping blindingly against the sides of my face, I saw… something. I wasn't sure what it was, but I didn't care, honestly, because I was about to die, and dying wasn't something I wanted to do. Whatever it was might not help, but it wasn't likely to be worse than dying by hitting the ground in another couple of seconds, so I reached for it. Grabbed at it. And felt somewhat gratified when my hand snagged around a feathered appendage. Then something shrieked like an angry eagle.

My momentum wrenched. I had been prepared for it, hoping for it even—not falling was my goal right now, so it didn't actually tear my arm out of its socket, though it sure felt like it was going to.

Beneath my grip I could feel feather, muscle, and bones shift, as my hand clutched the limb of whatever it was I was clinging to. Then I felt something sharp and awful tear at the skin on my upper arm, but I refused to let go, because FUCK that. I held on as tight as I could. Whatever I'd just grabbed onto WAS NOT FALLING. And not falling meant not dying, maybe, at least for a little while, and I was not about to let go of that.

Unless it cut off my arm.

Which it was clearly trying to do.

I screamed, and looked up again through a flash of flapping hair to see that the thing I had caught hold of was the thing that had been attacking Az and I. The same type of creature that had charged into me and Az to begin with. Possibly even the same one that had knocked me to my narrowly avoided death, but I couldn't be sure as I hadn't gotten a good look at the time.

I got a good look now, though; eagle wings and eagle legs from the knee down, but the upper body of a woman who clearly didn't think much of clothing and who definitely had a thing for weapons. Honestly, she seemed like the kind of person I'd have gotten along with pretty well, if she hadn't been so obviously trying to kill me. Call me cold, but I take exception to people trying to throw me to my death.

The eagle-woman had multiple blades sheathed on her person in thick baldrics that crossed at the center of her chest, more than one scabbard belted to her waist, and possibly another over her shoulder blades—she almost looked like a pin cushion with all the sword and dagger hilts poking out of her—but not a stitch of cloth or armor covered her breasts, waist, or head. I managed to get a good look at her, despite the blood splatter that was flying in my face from where she was trying to hack through my arm with a spear. Honestly, there wasn't much I could do other than stare at her while gripping her eagle leg for dear life, trying to grit through the pain of having my arm sliced repeatedly.

It must have been a terribly awkward angle for her. The spear was pretty long, and she still had it gripped for a more distant opponent, so she missed as often as she caught me, and rarely hit the same place twice. Perhaps she was just hoping to make me let go, rather than cut me all the way through the bone, but I wasn't planning to let go before I bled to death or she landed.

She cried out again, and this time some of her compatriots must have heard her, because I could hear answering cries from somewhere nearby. It was almost a surprise to be able to hear anything but the rush of wind in my ears, but as my "ride" seemed content to maintain altitude instead of plummeting us to the ground, or racing off across the countryside, other sounds were starting to filter in. Like the sound of metal slicing flesh every time the eagle-woman caught my arm with her spear, the subsequent gritted screams from my own lips, or the sounds of the other eagle-warriors' angry shrieks getting closer.

I had just begun to wonder why she wasn't just trying to spear me in the throat, when I saw the weapon drive towards my face. I barely managed to get my other arm up in time to block it. Of course, that arm took a deep gash as it deflected the spear tip—why wasn't I wearing bracers? I really needed to invest in a good pair of bracers—but the harpy, or eagle-woman, or whatever she was, was also slow enough in retracting the spear that I managed to get my hand wrapped around the shaft before she could pull it out of my reach.

And that whole exchange probably explained why she hadn't been aiming at my throat earlier.

You can bet your ass I pulled on that spear with all the force I could spare, which wasn't much, considering what my other arm was doing to keep me alive (holding my entire body weight, bleeding profusely, etc.), but apparently she had a bad grip on the thing to begin with, because my weak-assed yank was enough to pull it out of the harpy's hands.

"HA!" I yelled, as the spear came free of her grip. I was still in a damned precarious position, but at least I was now armed.

I twisted the grip of the spear as quickly as I could, flipping the shaft around in a single hand as if it were a bo, trusting in years of martial arts training to keep me from dropping the damned thing, so that the pointy end was now angled towards the harpy. She didn't seem to approve of that development, and she was damned quick to demonstrate her disapproval, because she met the spear point with the blade of a short sword she'd pulled from one of her many sheaths.

I don't know if she thought I'd actually intended to stab her—which would be a stupid move on my part, since she was the only thing keeping me from plummeting to my death right now—or if she was just still working on killing me, but either way she was clearly ready to cut me any way she could.

We'd barely had time to exchange a few blows, mostly me using the shaft of the spear to parry her attempts to cut my arm off, before something huge, black, and feathered crashed into both of us and knocked me loose.

"GwenDAMNit!" I screamed, as I began to fall again.

I'd barely dropped for more than half a second though, when a taloned claw grabbed me around the middle and I realized that what had barreled into us had been Azrael.

"Ok. Ow, and thank you," I half said, half screamed, as Azrael started a steep dive towards the forest that lay beneath us.

Something swished past my ear, and I turned to see a cloud of harpies flying above and behind us, launching various weapons in our direction.

We were so screwed.

Az was rocketing towards the trees below us, and I began to wonder if they were planning on slowing us down before we hit the trees, or the ground, or the whole cloud-of-harpies-below-us-fuck! Apparently, the dive was partially in order to blow through the harpies that had amassed between us and the tops of the trees. Trees that seemed much closer now than they had only five seconds earlier. Suddenly, my vision went almost black and my world became a haze of wings, talons, and branches. I couldn't see what I was doing really, but I swung out blindly with my newly acquired spear a few times, just in case any of the harpies tried to attach themselves to us as we dropped. The cries that I heard even as we plummeted through the cloud of winged warriors gave me a sense of grim satisfaction. I still had no idea what had sparked the ire of these people to begin with, but I did not take kindly to people trying to kill me, no matter what their reasoning might be.

Just before we crashed into the forest floor, Az spread their wings and cut our speed by at least half, but we still hit with a jolt that shook every bone in my body, especially since Az had needed to drop me before slamming their feet into the ground. I rolled away from the massive raven, over soft earth and a thick layer of pine needles, and stood up, shaken, dirty, and bleeding, but already brandishing the spear I'd somehow held onto through our entire crazed descent, ready for whatever came at us next.

Which was, of course, more harpies.

Despite everything we'd just gone through, we'd only disabled one or two of them, and that left more than a dozen who were still all too eager to take us down. Thankfully, the dense tree-tops slowed their descent, and spread them out.

Sadly, that didn't leave us any less outnumbered.

Az seemed to be stuck in raven form, and as far as I could tell, they didn't have access to any of the powers that had allowed them to kick so much vampire ass on Earth. I had nothing more than ten years of martial arts training and a spear I'd never used before. From what I could make out in the shadows of the dense pine forest, we were up against more than a dozen armed warriors, and we would be totally and completely fucked once they had us surrounded.

Which would be in about 30 seconds.

"Well, Az, it has been a pleasure knowing you," I said, shifting my stance so that we were back to back. "Shame we couldn't enjoy a longer association."

Caw.

I couldn't be sure, but that had sounded like it held a sincere tone of regret.

The harpies—my years of reading fantasy novels made me want to call them harpies, and eagle-women was getting tiresome, so, accurate or not, I was going to call them harpies—were landing all around us, and though they didn't seem to be as nimble on the ground as they were in the air (they hopped awkwardly to move themselves forward rather than walking like any biped I was familiar with), they still seemed more than adequately equipped to kill us both and have time for coffee after.

"We'll take as many as we can with us, though, right?"

Caw.

It was nice not to be alone, in one's final moments. I took a deep breath and widened my stance. I was going to make these assholes come to me.

One of the harpies shrieked, in what I took to be a battle cry, but then the one immediately in front of me, the one closing in that I had assumed would be my first opponent, turned to look at whoever had cried out.

I didn't hesitate. I lunged forward with my spear, taking the opening to stab for the harpy's chest. She turned back just before I connected, and brought her sword up in time to deflect the spear into her shoulder. I was shocked when the spear tip simply bounced off of her bare skin as if it were actually platemail.

My assessment of how screwed we were went up a few notches.

At least, it did until the shrieks that I'd been hearing all around us, shrieks that I'd assumed were harpy battle cries—you know, getting pumped to destroy two unarmed combatants who had no idea why they were even under attack, as you do—abruptly fell silent. I had just enough time to find that totally eerie before the harpy standing in front of me was no longer in front of me, but instead pinned to the nearest tree by what looked like nothing more than a grey haze.

"Did you want this one?" asked a raspy voice I didn't recognize.

I blinked, and the outline of a small figure came into focus in the midst of the haze. I said nothing, and the voice must have taken that as a "no," because the next thing I knew there was a sickening crack and the harpy collapsed to the ground.

In the sudden silence of the forest, I blinked and looked around. Harpy bodies lay everywhere, and not one of them was moving. Whatever the grey haze was, it had taken out every single one of our opponents singlehandedly.

U NSURE OF WHETHER or not we were actually safe now, I turned to look at Azrael. They stood abnormally still beneath the hulking pine trees, which cast us in enough shadow that it was difficult to be certain it was still daylight, even though it had clearly been close to midday when we had been up above the trees less than three minutes ago. Amid the smell of pine needles and some sweet-smelling sap, Az stood blinking their large raven eyes, as if they were still trying to adjust to a change in light.

I was about to laugh with relief when Azrael's legs seemed to give out from under them. I ran to their side.

"Az, are you alright?" I asked, kneeling beside the enormous raven.

Caw.

I was not reassured by the weakness of Az's voice.

"Its wing is hurt," said the same raspy voice that had asked me if I wanted the final harpy.

I turned and found what looked like a twelve-year-old girl staring at me from a meter away. She was lithe, and had long flowing hair, but that was all I could really see about her. She was enveloped in a continuously shifting haze, or maybe she was just standing in her own personal sandstorm. I couldn't see all of her at once, and everything about her was an uncertain shade of grey. Despite that, some part of her seemed eerily familiar.

"I wasn't quite fast enough," the girl said. "One of the harpies got to the raven before I could stop her."

Caw.

Azrael seemed to be agreeing with the girl.

Could this petite creature actually have killed over a dozen harpies in a minute? I wondered. I shook my head at that line of thought. Whatever she looked like, she was dangerous. Looks were deceiving enough, even back on Earth, and here? Well, Az was a giant raven instead of a squirrel or an angel, so… I had no clue what the rules were like here.

"Thank you for your help," I said. Then, turning to Az, "Can you show me where it hurts?"

Az turned a bit towards me and I realized that the wing they had been facing away from me was all but snapped.

"Shit," I said, sucking in a breath. I immediately began to search for splinting materials on the forest floor, and was exceedingly grateful, not for the first time, that I had taken more than one wilderness first aid course since I'd started high school.

Luckily, the forest floor was littered with long, straight branches from the tall pines that surrounded us, and it was warm enough here that I felt comfortable shedding the black leather jacket that had materialized with me the last time that I'd shifted. It was just barely large enough—when tied to one of the leather belts I'd taken off of a fallen harpy—to make a supportive sling and splint combo for Az's wing. I'd had to use my T-shirt as a bandage for my own arms, both of which were bleeding quite a bit more than I would have liked.

"Well," I said, looking between Az's ramshackle sling and my recently reduced ensemble. "Neither of us is going to be winning any fashion contests today, but at least you won't be in quite as much pain, and I still have a sports bra on."

Caw.

"You're right. I could do a decent Lara Croft cosplay right now."

The raspy voice chuckled, and I looked at the warrior girl who'd just saved our lives. As the hazy grey that shrouded her swirled around, I briefly caught a good look at her eyes. Then I felt a gasp escape me, when I realized what looked familiar about her. I'd seen those startling blue eyes before, more times than I cared to remember, most recently just before they'd been engulfed in flames.

"Renata?" I asked, amazed that my mind could conjure up a name I'd only heard mentioned once, in a conversation that felt like it had happened a year ago, though it had only been a matter of weeks.

Before I could take the breath to form a follow-up question, I found myself pinned to a nearby pine tree, with no idea how I'd gotten there except that there was now a small hand holding me by the throat and a swirl of grey mist in front of me.

"Did he send you?" the raspy voice asked from within the mist.

I wouldn't have known who the hell she was talking about except that the entire reason I'd recognized her was because she had her father's eyes.

"No, he didn't send me," I replied, as calmly as I could given my position. I was impressed that I was still able to speak over her grip around my throat, especially since I was also pinned to the tree. How strong was this creature, that she could hold me up by my throat without crushing it?

She eyed me for a full minute, while Azrael let out a series of startled and pleading caws, and I felt fairly certain that if this tiny person decided she didn't trust me, I would be dead and there would be nothing anyone could do to stop it.

"Why are you here, then?" she asked, eventually.

"Look, Renata, I'm not even entirely sure where here is, but Azrael and I were just trying not to get killed by a demon stampede when we landed in a field of wheat not far from here. As to your dad… when was the last time you had any news about him?"

I would have swallowed after asking, but Renata's grip tightened on my throat after I mentioned her father.

"Weeks ago, right after your friends deposited all of us in Unterberg."

So, she had recognized me from our rescue at Bolivia's MOME headquarters. I tried to take a deep breath, but mostly choked on my own spit. Renata loosened her grip marginally.

"If you know who I am," I began, once I'd stopped coughing, "then why would you think I was here at your dad's behest?"

Renata snorted and then spat on the ground.

"You wouldn't be the first beautiful woman whose head was turned by a vampire."

I laughed, and then choked a bit more, because it's hard to laugh when someone is holding you by the throat.

"You really don't know who I am, then," I said, still coughing. Renata dropped me and stepped back from both me and the tree.

"Explain yourself," was all that she said.

"First of all, before you worry about me being here on Edik's behalf, let me be the first to inform you that he is dead."

I wasn't one hundred percent certain that sharing that news with Renata would help things. It could turn out her love-hate relationship with her father was complicated enough that she would be quite upset to find out he was no longer among the living, but I got the distinct impression she wasn't going to be too cut up about it.

"Are you certain? Vampires are very difficult to kill," she said, and I could have been imagining it, but I thought her voice sounded… hopeful.

"Yeah, I learned that the hard way, but I am quite certain. He's dead."

"What happened to him?" she asked.

"Well, first a succubus ripped his head off," I explained. "But he was close to the Tree of Life when it happened, so it didn't stick, as it were. The next time I saw him, he attacked my brother, so I ripped his head off again and then had a dragon hit it with fire."

It was basically the truth. I was the dragon that had hit it with fire, so it was slightly misleading, but… well, I wasn't sure I wanted Renata to know all of my tricks. After all, I had no idea who, if anyone, she reported to.

I was bracing myself for some rage, or at least some verbal abuse for killing her dad. It even occurred to me that she might just straight up kill me, as she'd done with all the harpies who still littered the forest floor.

Without warning, I felt myself pushed against the base of the tree again, heard Azrael's startled caw as I felt the bark carve into my back, and expected that to be my final moment of existence.

Instead, I found a pair of lips pressed enthusiastically up against my own.

WHEN THE LIPS finally pulled away from mine, I dropped back to the forest floor and coughed again, mainly to cover the flush that had gone to my cheeks. I was not at all sure how I felt about being kissed by a woman who looked like a twelve year old, even if the chances were good she wasn't what she seemed. Icky probably summed it up, but damned if I was about to say that to Renata. So, I inspected the pine needles at my feet and coughed some more, while she gave me some space.

"I am free," she said, her voice full of wonder. "I am finally, truly, free of him. Thank you. I am in your debt."

I brought my eyes up and waved my hands in the kind of gesture one might make to calm a rearing horse.

"I don't think you owe me anything for killing your dad," I said.

"I humbly disagree. You have no idea what a nightmare he has made my life for the past few decades. Please, allow me to accompany you to the citadel. That's where you're headed, isn't it?"

I looked between Renata and Azrael. Azrael gave a slight nod, which I took to mean they thought we should accept the offer, but truth be told, I didn't particularly want to travel with Renata. She was… disconcerting at best, and… well, I didn't think there was anything I could do to stop her from kissing me again, or killing me, if she wanted to, and I didn't like feeling defenseless. So, I shrugged.

"I mean, we had planned to just take the same seam that brought us here and go back to the realm we came from, so——"

"Ah, no wonder the harpies set upon you! You cannot use any of your magic here without express permission from Hel."

"Hel?"

Renata quirked a smoky eyebrow at me and for the first time I wondered why she constantly looked like she was walking through a grey and swirling mist.

"Are we in another hell dimension?" I asked.

Renata shrugged.

"All the realms seem like hell realms if you ask me, but this one is ruled by a being named Hel."

"Like the Norse goddess?" I asked.

Renata shrugged.

"Perhaps? My Earth folklore is not what it could be."

I sighed.

"So... are you saying we wouldn't be able to use the seam, even if we managed to get back to it without being skewered by a bunch of harpies?"

Renata nodded.

"It is not that you cannot use it without your powers, since one does not need powers to access a seam, it is that Hel will not allow anyone to access the seam without her express permission. The same is true of using your own power. If you wish to return to where you came from by seam or by magic, then you have to go to the citadel. Hel awaits everyone who comes to her realm there."

Renata seemed to sense my hesitation and she rushed to reassure me.

"I was headed there anyway, it is hardly any trouble. I would be more than happy to ensure that you arrive there safely."

I sighed. I felt terrible enough for Azrael having a broken wing, just because it must've hurt like a bitch, but now I was doubly upset that the giant raven couldn't simply fly us to this citadel.

"How long will it take?" I asked, thinking of Siara sitting alone on that cliff, waiting for us. Thinking of Sol, Seamus, Rhelia, and Trev, all of whom probably thought I was dead, and knowing that every minute I was gone and they hadn't heard from me probably only confirmed their worst fears.

"Only a handful of days!" Renata said brightly, before flickering out of sight just as an arrow hit the ground where she'd been standing.

"Run, Victoria!" called the raspy voice in the mist, as more arrows thudded into the trees around us. I knew there was little I could do to help, and that Renata was clearly more than capable of taking care of herself. I would probably just get in her way. So, I did the only thing that made sense. I ran.

OF COURSE, I didn't get far before re-alizing that Azrael was going to need my help to get anywhere without tak-ing more than a healthy dose of ar-rows, so I slowed my own escape and focused on supporting the giant, hopping raven as they bounced between trees and over rocks, and gener-ally tried to avoid tumbling ass over teakettle down the steep slope we suddenly found ourselves de-scending.

The terrain in this realm changed so abruptly that if I didn't know better I would have thought it was altering just to spite us. I didn't have long to contemplate it, though, because even though we weren't running amid a hail of arrows anymore, the footing on this hillside was the exact combination of steep, rocky, and muddy that meant watching my footing was going to be key.

I'm not entirely sure what we would have done if Renata hadn't been there, but I'm pretty sure that the short answer is "died."

As it was, I kept an arm around Az to help them keep their balance on the side where their wing was tied up, and we ran/hopped as fast as we could down the slope while Renata killed all the things that were trying to attack us from behind.

I was becoming more and more curious as to just what a Damphir could do, as the sound of flying arrows faded and we came to a somewhat sudden stop. Unfortunately, I had other questions that I needed to address first.

Such as, "Where the fuck did this canyon come from?"

"My best guess would be erosion," replied the raspy voice behind me.

I would have laughed, but I was too busy being dumbfounded by how a canyon as large as the one that spread before us could have been impossible to see in the distance when we were in the air fifteen minutes ago and had a literal bird's eye view of the place. And I must have been dumfounded enough to say part of that out loud, because Renata replied in short order.

"It could be enchanted to be invisible from the air, or possibly even to move at Hel's discretion. This is a very strange realm."

"I thought this place suppressed magic. I can't access any of my powers," I said, my brows furrowed as I looked between Renata and the giant gap in the landscape that looked at least a kilometer wide.

"You cannot access your powers, but not because magic is suppressed here—simply because Hel does not permit its use."

"Well, how in the hells does she regulate that? It's not like you can take people's magic from them."

Renata quirked an eyebrow at me.

"Well, I cannot speak as to what anyone else can do, but in this realm, Hel absolutely takes people's power from them. She alone has the discretion to use her powers or not, as she sees fit, in the Realm of the Dead."

She looked out across the canyon and sighed.

"Regardless of how it appeared here, we will need to find our way around it. It may add some days to our journey."

A million questions swam in my head in that moment. How could anyone take someone else's power, how could anyone hide a whole fucking canyon, what did it mean that this was called the Realm of the Dead, and did it mean that I had died somehow? Also, how in the name of Gwen was I supposed to convince Hel to let me use my powers to get out of here? I took a deep breath and stilled them all, because in that moment only one thing really mattered. I looked out across the canyon again, and then bent over and crawled to the nearest ledge to check out our options.

"The fastest way past this thing is going to be across it rather than around it," I said. "It could take weeks to bypass it, but down and through… it should just take a couple of days."

I looked at the sun.

"We should descend almost to the bottom today, but not quite all the way. If days are the same length here that they are back home, or close to it, then we don't have enough sunlight to make it all the way across, and we don't want to risk sleeping on the bottom in case it rains in the night. Could be prone to flash floods. Tomorrow we hopefully cross the whole thing and then make our way up and out on the other side."

Renata looked at me, then at Azrael, then at the canyon one more time.

"What makes you think we can even cross it?" she asked. "There is no trail. No suggestion that other humans have been this way."

I smiled.

"No, but there is a goat trail, just over there." I nodded in the direction of the faint trace of a path a few meters away. "And we ought to be able to make that work."

Renata frowned.

"Goats are excellent climbers," she said.

"So am I," I replied, just before hopping over the edge to the aforementioned goat trail and offering a hand back up to Azrael.

Azrael looked at Renata, then at me, let out a non-committal caw, and extended their good wing down to where I waited on the rocks below.

Renata looked at me and shrugged before jumping down beside me.

THE NEXT FEW days were difficult. Az's wing was causing them all kinds of pain as we made our way down the loose, steep choss field that was the canyon wall, and every slip, stumble, and fall seemed to wear heavily on the poor, feathered mess.

Renata seemed as unfazed by our descent into the canyon as she was by everything else in life. She helped with Az sometimes, but mostly she just trailed behind us, silent, weaving in and out of the grey mist that surrounded her constantly.

Alone, crossing this canyon would have been a challenge, but with a giant injured raven in tow, the whole debacle felt like one monumental obstacle after another. And yet… and yet, for the first time in three weeks, I felt like I wasn't spinning completely out of control. I felt… grounded, solid, real. After weeks of being thrown one new magical conundrum after another, after trying to solve problems I hadn't even known existed before I was pushed head first into this crazy-assed ocean of magic in the midst of a fucking hurricane… it felt really good to just be in charge of getting three people from one side of a canyon to another.

Like, so good.

Like, even when I was trying to shove a busted raven over a four foot high ledge that was crumbling quickly all around us, or when I was traversing a twenty foot shelf that plummeted into a pool full of scummy water but which would allow me to meet the injured raven in a place that would help them overcome the next bit of cliff face with a much lower chance of dying, or while I was cleaning and cooking trout that Azrael had snatched from the river with their beak in order to feed us all, or building a fire with nothing but two sticks, a large piece of bark, some dry leaves, and a shit-ton of elbow grease, or falling asleep in a heap of raven feathers each night so exhausted that even the scars on my shoulder and face throbbed with it, even then, my days in the canyon seemed a thousand times more manageable than this whole take-down-the-corrupt-magical-government-before-it-takes-everyone-else-down-with-it schtick.

I mean, fuck, why couldn't more of my problems be solved just by managing to survive in the wilderness? This was what I was good at. This was what I had trained to do since I was a tiny kid. This was where I felt like, not only did I know my ass from a hot rock, but I could defend a doctoral thesis on the ways in which my ass differed from a sun-warmed piece of basalt.

So perhaps it should have been no surprise to anyone that when we finally clawed our broken, tired asses up to the top of the cliff on the far side of the canyon and saw a giant fucking mountain range full of jagged, snow-capped peaks in front of us, I just laughed, turned to help pull Az up over the ledge behind me, and kept on plowing ahead.

IF YOU'RE NOT familiar with traversing mountain ranges, you may not be aware that, unless you're on a trip with the specific goal of bagging a summit, you don't generally want to go over any mountain tops. You want to go between and around them as much as possible. Mountains can come in many shapes and sizes, and some of the really old ones can be pretty mellow, but young upstarts like the Rockies, Andes, and Sierras do not fuck around. The mountain range between us and this "Citadel" Renata kept referring to was new to me, but it looked young. Stark, steep, devoid of plant life from about two-thirds of the way up. It was an imposing line of stone sentinels that ran the length of the horizon, and stretched from the ground beneath our feet to the cloud cover that kept its peaks invisible.

In other words, it looked a lot like my old backyard.

Unfortunately, my old backyard regularly kills people. The Rockies aren't a great place to drag an injured friend around, and the pass we were going to need to clear here in the Realm of the Dead was not nearly as friendly as I would have liked either. The pass would keep us from having to summit any of the nearest peaks, but only by a few hundred meters. We still had quite the climb ahead of us. Unlike the canyon we'd just traversed, the pass at least did us the favor of having a trail winding up it. Sadly, that didn't help as much as one might hope. We still wound up having to scale a handful of giant boulders that lay across the switchbacks winding up the steep slope. We couldn't skirt the boulders without risking rolling a few hundred meters down the scree pile that called itself a mountainside here, so up and over we went.

All that scrambling made me extremely grateful that my arms had been healing well; the cuts and bruises that I'd entered the canyon with had stayed clean enough that they'd scabbed over well and could now withstand a bit of exertion. Even still, I had to grit through quite a bit more pain to get myself and Az up over those boulders than I would have liked.

The trail, such as it was, also meant that the aforementioned scree pile wasn't completely covered in a season's worth of cracked and shifting snow for every step of the way. Only half of the way. What can I tell you? Trails aren't always as useful as everyone wants them to be. Sometimes, all they do is tell you that someone else was once stupid enough to make your same mistakes.

On the other hand, the trail also did sweet fuck all to keep us from freezing to death as we fought gale force winds, driving snow, and ice-slicked crenellations on our way to the top of the saddle. As I shoved my hands under my armpits and jumped up and down in place while Renata helped Az over the last crusted rise that should lead to our descent, I reminded myself that this was better than the peaks to either side of us—which definitely would have killed us if we'd tried them—but it wasn't much better, and I was close to hypothermic by the time I'd dragged my own ass over the top.

Sadly, no matter how much I bitched under my breath, the weather didn't seem to be interested in our epic human vs. nature narrative thread, and the wind, clouds, and blowing snow kept the view at the top hidden from us. I could smell the ice-tinged air that often accompanied high altitude ascents, but I did not get to enjoy a sweeping view of the land below us, and I would have been pissed about it, but I was too busy trying to stay warm now that we were no longer climbing.

I had to do a lot of skipping to keep my blood pumping, and Az kept stopping to wrap me in their good wing periodically, shoving me up against their warm, feathered, bird body. Then, when we were about halfway through our descent, the view opened up. I might have missed it if Renata hadn't been there.

As it was, I had my head down and was grumbling, "What the hell is the point of being in a damned book if the clouds don't clear to let you enjoy an epic view from the summit of a mountain you just dragged a giant busted bird up, anyway? If I have to keep performing rescues that almost get me killed and I have to be rescued half the damned time even though I've been granted a bunch of ridiculous magical powers that are straight out of a completely predictable chosen-one narrative, shouldn't we at least get to enjoy the fucking view? Even the fucking hobbits got to enjoy the view, every now and again."

And then, suddenly, I ran into Renata, who had stopped dead on the narrow trail in front of me.

"What…" but as I raised my eyes from where the trail met Renata's mist-covered boots, I saw precisely what had made her stop. The sun, which had been hiding in the clouds for the past few hours of our journey, was now peeking out from behind its grey curtain to entertain us with a glorious orange, red, pink, and purple display splattered across the clouds. And the light show silhouetted the peaks and valleys of an enormous citadel that rested at the foot of the mountains we'd just crossed.

"Well, fuck me."

Caw.

"It is rather splendid in this light," Renata admitted.

“THAT'S ONLY A few hours away,” I said.

Renata nodded, or I thought she did. It was difficult to see a motion that subtle through the swirling grey mist that constantly surrounded her.

As we descended the remainder of the mountain in silence, half taken by the glorious sunset glowing ostentatiously behind the city in the distance, half consumed with thoughts of what getting to the citadel meant for each of us, I considered Renata's figure moving silently before me and wondered if the mist was some kind of magic, and, if so, how she managed to use it. After all, Az and I were unable to access any of our powers.

“It is not magic,” she said, over her shoulder in front of me.

"You can read minds now?" I was starting to wonder how much Renata wasn't telling us.

"You were going to ask me eventually," she said, as if that was a perfectly reasonable explanation.

"Care to explain how you know that?"

"The mist, how quickly I move, even my strength, all come from one simple thing," she explained. "I am only half in this realm, and always half in my own realm."

My brain stuttered.

"How does that work?"

"I am not entirely sure of the science behind it. It is not widely studied, as my kind are incredibly rare, but something about my existence creates a permanent portal between my realm and whichever other realm I choose to travel in. However, time in my realm runs… differently, and… I can move back and forth in other realms' timelines with some flexibility. Which is why I appear to move faster than should be possible."

"And your strength?" I asked.

She shrugged.

"The gravity in my realm is considerably higher than in most other realms. Most realms leave me feeling feather light and as strong as a titan."

Caw.

I jumped forward to keep Azrael from running into me, and started walking again. My feet had apparently been unequal to the task of keeping me moving while my brain processed the information it had just gotten.

"How do you manage to exist in two places at once?" I asked, once my feet had started moving again.

"I am not sure. As I said, it is a little studied phenomenon."

Something about Renata's voice made me think she wasn't quite telling the truth, but maybe it was my imagination.

"It is why MOME was so desperate to capture and study me," she offered up after a long pause. "It is also why my father was so desperate to keep me near. He was…a peculiar vampire."

That sounded ominous enough that I was pretty much afraid to ask, but apparently I didn't need to. While Renata had been almost entirely quiet on our journey up to now—despite my many questions about this supposed "Realm of the Dead" and what it meant that we were here—she was suddenly all too willing to share. The drastic change was welcome, in a way. I knew so little about how this world worked that any new information seemed incredibly valuable to me, although it also made me a bit uncomfortable.

"I believe you are familiar with my father's obsession with me?" she asked.

"Sort of," I said. "He was very keen to get ahold of you. It was why he kept trying to give us over to MOME. Or at least, he was always asking me where you were whenever he showed up with a bunch of MOME asshats trying to kill us."

"And you did not simply tell him where I was and leave me to my fate?"

I thought about that for a minute. It would have been easier to tell Edik where we'd left Renata and let them have their own showdown, but…

"All I knew about you was that you had been rescued with the rest of the 'child' captives held with MOME and that you clearly hadn't tried to get in touch with your dad after getting free. I knew we'd left instructions with the folks caring for all the children to put them in touch with their families if they wanted them. I figured if you hadn't tracked down Edik yet, there was a reason. And, after my own experiences with him, I wasn't keen to force him on anyone else."

"Most people on Earth would have insisted that a child should be reunited with their parents," Renata commented, seemingly without ire.

"Well, I'm not most people. There are good reasons for kids not to want to be with their parents. If you'd been younger, I might have arranged a meeting or something. I think that's what they did for all the youngest kids we busted out of MOME, but older ones…"

Renata laughed, a dry sound, at least in this realm.

"I am certainly older. I am likely twice your age, at least in your world. However, in my world… I do not seem to age in my world. And as I spend more than half my time here… I do not seem to age very quickly at all. I believe that is why my father wished to find me. He was rather… obsessed with his own mortality."

"Uh… wasn't he a vampire?"

"Indeed. He was. But did you know that vampires aren't truly immortal?"

That had me stopped in the trail long enough for Az to smack into my back.

Caw.

"They aren't?" I asked.

Renata laughed again.

"Oh, they are so close as for it to make no difference to most of them. With food in abundance, they will live for thousands of years. No one is entirely sure quite how long. But eventually, their bodies can no longer support the constant energy transfer, so they age and die, just like anyone else."

"So… you're telling me Edik was afraid of dying?"

"Indeed. So much so, that he was willing to spend as much time as possible in my realm with me. He was convinced it would stop his aging."

"Woah, so he was going to what, move in with you?"

"In a sense…. I do not think that would have worked, for many reasons. But he was determined to try. I could never be near him but he would find a way to latch on to me and make me take him into my own realm."

We were all silent for a long time, as we resumed our slow plod down the steep hillside.

"I do not enjoy having other people in my realm. It… feels wrong."

And sure, I could see that. I mean, I didn't have my own pocket realm that I could visit at will, but… I didn't even like having most people hang out in my room for too long. If I had a whole realm that was unique to me, and I was forced to share it against my will?

I shuddered.

I decided not to ask too many follow-up questions on that one, though. Honestly, I was amazed with how much information Renata had just volunteered. No one else in the magical community had been this forthcoming with me. Then again, maybe this was just the first chance I'd had to spend time talking to someone about how any of this stuff worked. It seemed like ever since that first night that Edik had attacked me, the night when Seamus had explained a bit about being a werewolf and I'd first learned that magic was more than something to read about in books, I'd been constantly on the run, trying to preserve my life and the lives of everyone I cared about. It had all been running, evading capture, dodging death, helping people, getting rescued, almost dying…. None of which left time for lectures about how magic worked, what everything was called, or who got which powers, and why.

Which reminded me…

"Hey, Az, I've been meaning to ask. Do you have different preferred pronouns for your different forms?

Caw caw.

On our first night camping in the canyon, we'd decided two caws would be no. One would be yes. Charades was even harder for Az in crow form than it had been as a squirrel demon.

"So, if I use they/them for all of your forms, that's ok with you?"

Caw.

"Is there any time you'd like me to use different pronouns?"

Caw caw.

"Cool. Sorry I didn't ask earlier. Everyone just keeps trying to kill us and then I forget."

Caw.

Az's beak lowered to my shoulder and they nipped very gently at my earlobe in what I took to be an affectionate motion. It still hurt. I tried to be surreptitious about rubbing it after they let go, though.

I looked out at the citadel in the distance again, and the excitement I'd felt at first seeing it—knowing the end of our journey was in sight, that I'd soon have my powers restored and be able to get back to fighting MOME and stopping Rebecca Dryer from blowing up the world—faded, as I realized that as soon as we reached that citadel, we'd be out of the wilderness and I would be back to feeling like I'd stumbled into the chat room for a MMORPG as a level one character, while the only other people logged in were level 70 and all in a different guild than me.

"Do not worry, Victoria," Renata said, ignoring the hundred times that I'd asked her to call me Vic. "You will not feel like a fish out of water forever. Soon you will hit your stride."

I laughed awkwardly, deciding that even if what Renata could do wasn't mind reading, it was close enough to make me uncomfortable.

This time when the citadel caught my eye, I began wondering how different things would be there compared to all of the other magical places I'd been so far. It looked… like the silhouette of a life-sized Duplo construction—as though a mountain-sized toddler had spent hours perfecting their sprawling structure, half blocky towers, half single-story sprawls, none of it particularly artfully put together, though still striking when haloed by the setting sun from a great distance.

"It does not improve upon closer inspection," said Renata, putting the final nail in the coffin of "I'm not mind reading."

"But I am not," she said. "It is only that once I have responded to something you were going to say in a moment, you will not say it anyway, and so you believe you only thought it."

"So what about the times where I do speak first?" I wondered aloud.

"People are often disturbed by this habit of mine, so I try to keep myself in their time stream as often as I can," she replied. "But I am scouting ahead to make sure that we aren't running into trouble, and I cannot help what I overhear when I return."

"Ugh…" I muttered. "Time travel makes my brain hurt."

Renata turned to me then.

"It is not time travel, it is two realms moving at different speeds through the universe and occasionally touching. Time travel is—"

"If you're going to tell me time travel isn't possible I am going to laugh in your face," I said, before she could finish.

The petite young woman—I had rather resolutely decided that no matter how young she looked, someone who had killed as many people as she had couldn't be considered a child—stared at me with blue eyes that reminded me far too clearly of her dad, and a shiver went down my spine despite my best efforts to look resolute.

"You sound awfully certain for someone who is so new to this world of magic," she said, in a tone that suggested I was insane.

"I may have only just joined this world where dark matter can bend reality, but… let's just say, I've been getting a crash course in what's possible."

Renata considered me for a moment, walking backwards down the trail as she did so, and causing me no small amount of angst as I worried that she'd take a step too far to either side and go tumbling down the side of the mountain.

Then she simply turned on her heel and continued on in silence.

Caw, said Az.

"Caw indeed," I mumbled.

~~~

By the time we reached the citadel my dislike of this realm had gone from mild to emphatic. Aside from the harpies that had tried to kill us right after we'd stepped through the seam to get here, the changing landscape that seemed custom designed to slow us on our journey, and the fact that Az and I couldn't access any of our powers, the city itself had slowly resolved into precisely what it had appeared to be from afar.

It was a life-sized Duplo construction designed and executed by a toddler. Only it wasn't the vivid primary colors that a Duplo set boasted, but rather a combination of concrete and plastic blocks in a dull series of greys and tans that gave the impression of a sepia photograph of soviet Russia.
~~~

Consequently, I wasn't even surprised when, as we tiredly stumbled our way up to a tall grey wall topped with medieval looking spikes that had no business in a Duplo set, a horde of harpy guards descended from atop the wall, rushed us with spears, and informed us that we were to be taken straight to Hel.

"AH, YES. WELCOME back, Renata, darling. You've done well."

I glared around the massive hall that we'd just been prodded into. Harpy spears, as I'd learned on my first day in this shitty realm, were quite sharp, and I cannot tell you how little I appreciated being jabbed at with them for the entire three kilometer long walk that stood between the wall where we'd been apprehended and the hall that housed the ruler of the Realm of the Dead.

So, while I normally might have been quite impressed with the vaulted ceiling that crowned a chamber that had been studiously transformed from concrete block (which it had clearly been on the outside) to cavern-like structure of hedonistic pleasure, I was decidedly not in the mood by the time we got there.

There were steaming pools in every direction I looked, all filled with naked people of every variety. The diversity of bodies on display (in terms of size, shape, skin and fur colors, numbers of horns, eyes, and extra limbs) was equal to that of the crowded streets of Unterberg. Here, however, there was decidedly less clothing involved in the equation, and quite a bit more steam. The misty pools of naked people were spread evenly about the room/cavern/whatever this was, but terraces gradually raised the elevation a half meter at a time until the whole thing plateaued at a terrace covered in a series of boulders shaped into a throne. Atop the throne sat a scantily clad blue-skinned woman with eight arms.

"I thought you hailed from Norse mythology," I said aloud, before I could think better of it. We had been dragged before the eight-armed figure, on the next terrace down, and forced to our knees by the harpies who had wrangled us this whole way, and my tendency to fight emotional overload with snide commentary seemed to be as strong as ever.

I was pissed about a few things, not least of which was that it sounded like Renata had been working with this blue-skinned deity to bring us here, and when I'm angry, I get surly. You may have noticed.

"Tsk, tsk, Victoria, I'd been led to believe you were intelligent," replied Hel.

The silence that followed was clearly meant to give me time to piece together all that was wrong with my assumptions, so I stared at the goddess for a minute before shrugging.

"My Hindu pantheon is pretty limited, sorry."

In reply, the blue figure stuck out her tongue, long and red with blood, and then she shifted to a form that was similar to the first but entirely black instead of blue, and added quite a few more heads and arms than I could count in the few seconds she held it. Then she shifted back to blue, with four arms. Which was when my world religions class from sophomore year poked my brain a few times, and it finally clicked.

"Oooh! Kali! Nice. I guess that makes sense. I'm not super familiar with the mythology, but there's something in there about the realm of the dead, isn't there? So you and Hel…" my voice trailed off as the deity shifted to a tall, lithe, fair-haired, blue-eyed white lady.

"I am Hel, and many others besides," she said, filling the silence that I'd left, and indeed, filling the cavern with the resonance of her voice.

"Cool. Well, whatever you wanna call yourself is fine by me, but I am mainly concerned with getting the Hell out of here (pun intended), so if you could just give me my powers back…"

The woman laughed and shifted back to the blue-skinned, four-armed version of herself, and I blinked hard to keep the dizziness at bay. It was kind of like looking at Azrael when I couldn't get one form to hold, but there must have been something else about Hel's power that made my head spin, because she was only taking one form at a time.

"You are in my realm now, Victoria, and you will do as I require," she said, placing one set of hands on her hips and crossing the other set in front of her chest.

"Look, I appreciate that this is your place, and I really appreciate the hospitality of a few dozen harpies trying to kill me the moment I arrived, but I'm going to have to pass on whatever else you're offering."

I held the deity's gaze, even though her eyes were difficult to focus on, and I knew I was pushing my luck a lot farther than was wise. What can I tell you, my fear response is sass.

"No one leaves this realm without my consent, and none may use power save at my discretion," she hissed. "Everyone completes a task for me. Renata here retrieved you and brought you to my doorstep, as she was bid."

She gestured towards the ball of grey mist that obscured Renata, now quite a bit thicker than I had ever seen it, almost thick enough to block out Azrael's giant crow form standing behind her, but I still managed to make out that Renata's hands were no longer bound. The thought that Renata might have set us up angered me, but right now it was taking a back seat to a hundred other rage inducing thoughts, so I quickly turned back to the four-armed woman in front of me.

"Look, I appreciate that you enjoy a good power trip. Totally understandable, especially if you live forever and get bored easily, but if I don't get back to my own realm as soon as possible, there may not be much of this realm or any other left, and I don't have time to—"

"You will do as you are told, or suffer the consequences!"

And with that, all four of Hel's hands snapped their fingers and two people were suddenly standing beside her that I'd never expected to see again. I recognized them even from afar, even with clouds of steam wafting between us. I would recognize them anywhere.

"Vic?" asked my mother.
"Vic?" echoed my dad.

"MOM?" I ASKED, my legs buckling beneath me as I looked from her to the man she was clinging to as if her own legs could barely hold her. "Dad?"

My world tunneled down to enclose only the two of them, the rest of the cavern's steaming pools and dark architecture fading from view, the smell of warm bodies and wet rocks dissolving as well.

My voice was barely a whisper now, but it echoed through the rocky chambers and I knew that they'd both heard me call them. My parents and I both lunged towards each other at the same time, but the harpies holding me pulled my rope-bound wrists backwards and I sank back to my knees even while Hel made a mere gesture that held my parents by some invisible force.

"What are my parents doing here? Why did you take them?" I growled, turning back to Hel.

"They came to me of their own volition, I assure you," Hel said, her smile curling into something almost feline, and in no way amiable. "They met the criteria, so they were permitted entry. What better place to hide, after all, than the Realm of the Dead?"

It felt like being stabbed, seeing my parents so close, yet completely out of reach, and hearing that they'd left me voluntarily. I looked at both my parents and saw the truth there. The flash of guilt in my Mom's eyes, the sadness in my dad's. Hel wasn't lying. They had come here of their own accord.

"Now," continued Hel, that same smile still curling the corner of her blue lips. "Everyone who comes to my realm must pay the price of admittance. You and your crow both meet the criteria, but that is not enough. You must complete a quest of my choosing, and then we will discuss the return of your powers, and the possibility of your being permitted to leave this place."

I still don't know if it was the surprise of seeing my parents alive, the torment of having them so close and yet not being able to hug them, ask if they were ok, and take them home, or just the blind rage at how fucking unfair everything had been for so long, but something inside of me simply snapped.

"No."

I said it quietly, but in that moment it might as well have been a scream.

"No?" asked Hel, the predatory smile falling from her lips. "What do you mean no? Do you realize what I could do to you?"

And as she asked, fire leapt to life all around me, scorching my skin and hair, and beginning to burn the rope that bound my wrists. It was hot, painfully so, but I was beyond caring. I just glared, and let the rage consume me in even greater measure than the fire.

"I don't care what you do to me," I said, realizing the words were true only as I spoke them. It wasn't that I wanted to die, far from it, it was just that I was so consumed with rage that I wanted to destroy everything, and didn't care if I took myself down with the ship. "I have been doing my damnedest, for weeks, to save Earth, the people I love, and the rest of the universe from a lunatic, and I do not have time for your bullshit quests. I do not have time for your weird ego trip, for your power hungry kleptomania, for whatever bullshit made my parents run to you, or whatever you want to threaten to do to them to try to gain my compliance."

I took a deep breath, ignored the heat that singed my nose hair, and got ready to speak again. It was like I'd broken a dam inside me and now nothing could stop it but getting the rage out. And there was… just so damned much of it. Who knows, a few weeks ago I'd probably have kept it all to myself and just played along. I'd certainly let everyone else tell me what was what ever since I'd learned that the world didn't work the way I thought it did. This rage in me had been building up ever since my parents had "died," and even more since I'd learned the truth about Trev, my powers, and everything else, but I doubt I would have let it loose like this—on someone who could probably destroy me with the snap of her fingers, no less—if I hadn't spent the past five days remembering that there were a few things in the universe that I did understand. A few things I'd worked hard to become competent at, and damn it all, I'd just led an injured raven the size of a small car through a canyon as big as the largest on Earth, and then between two mountains big enough to sit comfortably in the Rockies. I'd dealt with more shit than was reasonable already, and I was fucking bone tired of being told what to do by mystical people who called themselves gods, whether they were on my side or not.

"My parents fucking lied to me for ten years and then disappeared without me to save their own skins. I don't fucking care if you set them on fire right now. I've believed them dead for most of a year now, it won't be that much more crushing to see them actually dead. I have been tested, again and again, over the past few weeks, playing by a set of rules I've never been told, with a hand I can't even stop to look at, and I have no fucking clue who you are or why you think you have a right to anyone else's dark matter just because they wind up in your realm. But I will fucking tell you this right now, if you try to make me go on another fucking quest I will fight you with every Gwendamned thing that I am, and I don't care if it destroys me, your entire realm, and my parents too. There will be no quest. I have saved the world twice in the past week and I need to get home so I can do it again. And if that's not enough for you, then you deserve to go up in flames with the rest of the universe when Rebecca Dryer implodes it all in her misguided attempt to bring the non-magical world to heel."

Then I sat down on the ground, cross legged, in the ring of fire that was licking violently at my entire body and added, "and I will sit here and slowly burn to death until you make up your mind about how you feel about that, and everyone else can just fuck right off."

I WASN'T BLUFFING, exactly. I was so damned angry in that precise moment that I really didn't care if the whole world burned, and by the time I was done talking, the rage inside of me was burning so hot that I barely felt the ring of flames that licked at me as I collapsed into a lotus position on the floor of the cavern. I was even numb to the cry my mother let out when I sank down into the flames. In fact, hearing my mother's despair only fueled my rage. If she was so damned concerned for my well-being, why had she abandoned me, abandoned Trevor, left everything behind and just disappeared? What the hell were my parents playing at? They'd been dead to me for months, and now they were back and I was supposed to care enough about them to abandon the people back on Earth who had NEVER LEFT ME BEHIND just to save them?

Fuck that.

Fuck all of this.

"You are foolish, human, if you think your tantrum sways me at all," said Hel, although the flames surrounding me died away as she said it, so I wasn't sure how much truth was behind those words.

But then the same ring of fire enveloped my parents, and it took every shred of self-control I had not to launch myself at the blue-skinned goddess holding them hostage.

"If your own wellbeing doesn't convince you that your will is mine, then perhaps you need some external motivators."

I was still angry with my parents. Furious, really, even though part of me thought that might not be the most fair response to everything they'd likely gone through. But I pushed thoughts like that aside, focused on the rage instead, and stilled the part of me that was begging to be unleashed in some heroic attempt to save them. An attempt that would probably get me killed, or at the very least leave me stuck completing some stupid, arbitrary, waste of time, just to appease the whim of a goddess who got her jollies by stealing power and making people do things.

I didn't have time for that kind of bullshit.

So, I focused on my anger and ignored the part of me that still wanted to run to my parents' arms, or tear off the extra arms of the woman who was using them as bait.

I sighed and stood up again, not easy from a lotus position while my hands were bound, but I was still so angry I barely noticed the effort.

"You don't get it, do you? There will be nothing left for you to hoard if you don't let me get back to my friends. Your existence is as much at stake as mine. The weapon Rebecca Dryer plans to use will take out the entire universe. There will not be any realm that is spared. Anything that can be reached from Earth, or from an Earth-adjacent realm, all of it could be wiped out by a single use of this weapon. I have already wasted precious days scrambling across your ridiculous realm, dodging harpies, traversing canyons, and climbing mountains, but I refuse to waste another minute for your overinflated ego. And, I may be in a book, but damn it, I refuse, flat-out re-fucking-fuse to go on a side quest just because you have a hard on for pushing people around. If this damned author needs more words or something, they can fucking well figure out a plot twist that works, instead of sending me on a random adventure for no reason."

I took a deep breath and reminded myself that throwing insults around wasn't likely to get me anywhere. Egomaniacal tyrants didn't enjoy being insulted any more than most people did, probably quite a bit less, actually. Besides which, I probably wasn't convincing anyone of my sanity with the whole book rant. I tried changing tacks.

"I mean, look, it's not like I even know what the fuck I'm doing, really, when it comes to this whole saving the world business, but I just learned something that the folks on Earth really need to know if we're going to stop the madwoman with the evil plan, and I've already wasted…"

My voice trailed off as an idea struck me. Silence followed, probably because I sounded batshit nuts, not that I cared.

"Hel… How exactly is it that you take people's power here?"

Hel glared at me as if the question were incredibly rude.

"That is not an answer you've earned, human, that is—"

"Renata said you can choose who has their powers and who doesn't? Is that true?"

"No one accesses magic in this realm without my permission," Hel replied coolly.

"Right, so you can take away someone's power. Is it permanent?"

"That is none of your——"

"Could it be permanent?" I asked. "Could you strip someone of their power forever?"

Hel shrugged.

"All of this?" I gestured around the cavern that surrounded us, my brain putting things together, even in the face of Hel's reticence. "This was accomplished with the power of others, wasn't it? That's what feeds your power, right? Stripping it from everyone else here?"

Hel glared at me, but she didn't deny it.

"Look," I said, holding up my bound wrists in the best imitation of a gesture of surrender I could muster. "I don't care what you do with it, really, as long as it's possible that you can make it permanent."

Hel said nothing.

"I believe," I continued, hoping I was on the right track, "that if you assign me the quest of my choosing, I can bring you a power you might find quite useful."

Hel raised a single sculpted eyebrow and I decided now was my chance.

"In return for my completing a quest at the end of which I will deliver to you a mage of great power, all I ask is one favor in return. Deal?"

"And what quest would you choose, human?"

"Oh, you know, just overthrowing MOME, taking Rebecca Dryer permanently out of the game, and saving the universe."

I BLINKED AND rubbed my eyes, sure that I was imagining what I was seeing.

Because what I was seeing looked like every Gwedamned dragon in the dragon realm mustering for battle in the middle of a sun-soaked valley, and that... that didn't seem like the best idea, considering each and every one of them could be weaponized and used to take out... the world.

"What in the devil is going on here?" asked Azrael from beside me. They seemed relieved to be back in their succubus form, flaring their silver wings in the sunlight atop the pillar of earth on which we now stood, looking out over the dragon meeting grounds. Once Hel had agreed to my terms she'd been almost eager to get me out of her realm. She hadn't even let me say goodbye to my folks.

"I don't know, but I think we'd better find out before 'bad things' happen."

"Bad things?" Azrael raised an eyebrow, and I blinked hard as both of their forms tried to take up the same space in my vision. "Worse than the usual?"

"The same as usual," I replied.

Azrael just smiled and took wing—both of which were healed in their current form—and I was about to issue a complaint about them flying off without me, when I remembered that they weren't the only ones with wings.

I closed my eyes, calling to mind the feel of wind rushing over my scales, gravity defied by aerodynamics, and the faint trace of fire in my belly. Then I leapt off the ledge, spread my giant scaly wings, and joined Azrael as he spiraled down to the center of the frenetic bustle happening on the ground.

I shifted to my human form the moment we landed, and there was a moment of awkward silence before I was wrapped in more arms than I could easily count.

"Vic!"

"You're alive!"

"We thought—"

"When Az didn't come back right away—"

"No one knew—"

"How did you—"

I couldn't keep track of all the things being said at once, but tears flooded my eyes as I registered the familiar feel of everyone I'd thought I would die saving. Sol, Seamus, Trev, Rhelia… all there, all embracing me.

I'm so sorry, Vic, for everything before, about Rhelia.

I was too overwhelmed to reply, especially because something about Trev reaching out telepathically felt like regaining a limb I thought I'd lost, but all I could do was lean even harder into the group hug. It was probably minutes before any of us let go.

"Oh man," I said, wiping at my eyes. "I really missed you guys."

"You missed us?" Sol asked, sounding oddly surprised. When I turned to look at her, probably with confusion displayed in a twist of eyebrows, she smiled and shook her head. "I mean, that's fine, it's great that you care enough to miss us in a short period of time, but we were the ones that thought you were dead, Gatita. You knew you weren't dead. Why would you miss us? You've only been gone for a few hours."

I looked around at all of them, trying to catch the light in their eyes that would tell me Sol was fucking with me. I looked for Azrael to confirm that I wasn't losing my Gwendamned mind, but they were a few meters away talking intently with one of the dragons.

"Ok, this isn't funny," I said, my eyes snapping to Seamus, who I figured was the least likely to keep a joke running if it was clearly making someone uncomfortable, but he just looked at me with his head tilted to one side, as though waiting for an explanation.

"You guys, I was gone for like five days! What are you talking about?"

"Five days?" asked Trevor, looking concerned, but not nearly as incredulous as I would expect if I had seriously been gone for only a few hours here on Earth. "Which realm were you in?"

"Hell," I said, looking desperately between all the faces of the people I loved most in the world. "Or, well, the Realm of the Dead, not really Hell I guess, and not even really the Realm of the Dead, but that's what Hel called it, so…"

I trailed off, realizing that I was rambling. Sol looked curious, Seamus concerned, Rhelia looked… her face was oddly blank. Like blank enough that I was suddenly certain that she was hiding something, but before I could ask what that might be, Trev distracted me.

"Did you… meet anyone interesting there?" he asked, and the question snapped my attention back to him. As soon as my eyes met his, I knew. I knew in my bones, and the knowledge made me want to throw up.

"You knew they were there. This whole time. You knew."

The way Trev blanched, the tightness in his jaw, he looked almost like I'd punched him in the gut, and he didn't deny it, not even a little bit.

"Gatita, what—"

But I couldn't. I couldn't decide if it was worse that my parents had left without telling me where they were going, but had for some reason told Trev, or that Trev hadn't told me after he found out. It was hard to weigh betrayals that way.

I couldn't look Trev in the eyes, and I couldn't cope with feeling like I'd just gotten Trev back and then lost him again a few heartbeats later.

I wasn't really thinking of a destination when I reached through space and time, but I just didn't want to be here anymore, and I really hoped Azrael had been paying attention enough to fill everyone in on the pertinent details, because all I wanted to do was disappear.

Turns out that's a not a good mindset to have when one is reaching through spacetime.

When I opened my eyes, I was no longer surrounded by my friends, or hundreds of dragons preparing for battle.

I was no longer surrounded by anything at all.

Oops, I thought, as darkness enveloped me.

Vic's adventure concludes in Book 5 –
Victoria Marmot and the Road to Hell

If you somehow missed them, make sure you catch up with Victoria Marmot books one through three:

Victoria Marmot and the Meddling Goddess
Victoria Marmot and the Inconvenient Prophecy
Victoria Marmot and the Shadow of Death

Or collect them all in one place with:
Victoria Marmot the Complete Collection

Other works by Virginia McClain

The Chronicles of Gensokai Series:
  Blade's Edge
  Traitor's Hope

Short stories:
  Rain on a Summer's Afternoon

Follow Virginia on social media:
  www.virginiamcclain.com
  twitter.com/gwendamned
  facebook.com/virginiamcclainauthor

Acknowledgements

These books wouldn't have been possible without a fair bit of help from a number of people. My deepest gratitude goes out to the following people:

My editor, Aurora Wilson-McClain, for not only working with my sometimes ridiculous deadlines, but also for helping me sort out the best use of obscure spell references, the number of "s"s a certain dragon uses in her speech patterns, and where, exactly, everyone has left their clothes.

My husband, for putting up with me dis-appearing every evening for months on end in order to get these books written, for being my best cheerleader and for not giving me too much grief when I failed to get my half of the housework done.

Cedar, for letting me ignore her often enough to get formatting done, as well as promotion and marketing stuff, and for being so willing to hang out with her wonderful caregivers.

Anne, Lee, Jim, and Gabi, for keeping Cedar entertained, fed, and happy so that I could write.

To my proofreaders: Corey & Paul.

To my Patreon supporters: Paul, Corey, Mishy, Marie, and Jessica.

And finally, the folks at Stella's au CCFM for always putting up with me occupying a table for hours on end while only ordering a cup of tea.

Virginia McClain is an author who masqueraded as a language teacher for a decade or so. When she's not reading or writing she can generally be found playing outside with her four legged adventure buddy and the tiny human she helped to build from scratch. She enjoys climbing to the tops of tall rocks, running through deserts, mountains, and woodlands, and carrying a foldable home on her back whenever she gets a chance. She's also fond of word games, and writing descriptions of herself that are needlessly vague.

For more information check out
www.virginiamcclain.com
facebook.com/virginiamcclainauthor
twitter.com/gwendamned
bookbub.com/author/virginia-mcclain

www.ingramcontent.com/pod-product-compliance
Lightning Source LLC
Chambersburg PA
CBHW021317190726
48288CB00003B/870